DON'T STAY UP LATE

Also by R. L. Stine

R. L. STINE

DON'T STAY UP LATE

A **FEAR STREET** NOVEL

THOMAS DUNNE BOOKS
ST. MARTIN'S GRIFFIN
NEW YORK

THOMAS DUNNE BOOKS.
An imprint of St. Martin's Press.

DON'T STAY UP LATE. Copyright © 2015 by Parachute Publishing, LLC. All rights reserved. Printed in the United States of America. For information, address St. Martin's Press, 175 Fifth Avenue, New York, N.Y. 10010.

www.thomasdunnebooks.com
www.stmartins.com

Library of Congress Cataloging-in-Publication Data

Stine, R. L.
    Don't stay up late : a Fear Street novel / R. L. Stine.—First edition.
        p. cm.
    ISBN 978-1-250-05162-2 (hardcover)
    ISBN 978-1-4668-6674-4 (e-book)
    [1. Babysitters—Fiction. 2. Nightmares—Fiction. 3. Hallucinations and illusions—Fiction. 4. Monsters—Fiction. 5. Horror stories.] I. Title.
    II. Title: Don't stay up late.
    PZ7.S86037Ds 2015
    [Fic]—dc23

                                                            2014041171

St. Martin's Griffin books may be purchased for educational, business, or promotional use. For information on bulk purchases, please contact the Macmillan Corporate and Premium Sales Department at 1-800-221-7945, extension 5442, or write to specialmarkets@macmillan.com.

First Edition: April 2015

10 9 8 7 6 5 4 3 2 1

For Jane, who knows what's right

PART ONE

1.

My name is Lisa Brooks and I'm a twisted psycho. I wasn't always a total nutcase. Before the accident, I thought I was doing pretty okay.

My family moved to Shadyside in February. It took a little while to adjust to a new house, a new town, and a new high school. That's normal, right?

I had some hard times. I was lonely at first. I missed my friends back in Shaker Heights. Shadyside High was big and confusing, and most everyone I met had been going there forever and already had a group of friends.

I'd walk down the long halls to class, and everyone was laughing and talking, and sometimes I felt as if I didn't exist. I'm a little shy, and it's not easy for me to go up to someone I don't know and just start talking. So I felt kind of invisible my first few weeks there.

But by April, I was beginning to feel at home. I was making friends. Saralynn O'Brien and I were hanging out a lot. We seemed to have the same sense of humor and the same bad attitude about guys and school. We both thought high school was basically a crock—something you had to get through so your real life could start. And we both thought guys were an inferior species, inferior but necessary.

Yes. Necessary. I even had a boyfriend by April. Nate Goodman. I met him when I walked out of the cafeteria, bumped him from behind at the top of the stairs, and sent him tumbling headfirst to the bottom. I had my eyes on my phone and didn't even see him.

Luckily, Nate is a pretty slick acrobat. He managed to somersault most of the way. He had a few cuts that were bleeding a little, but he didn't break his neck.

Of course I went tearing down the stairs to make sure he was okay. He sat there shaking his head. I think he was dazed a little. I huddled over him. "Are you okay?"

"I was better a few seconds ago," he said.

I apologized at least a hundred times and helped pull him to his feet. I felt terrible. At least a dozen kids stopped to stare at us.

He wiped blood off his forehead with the back of his hand.

"Did you break anything?" I asked.

"Yes. The land-speed record for stair falling," he replied.

"I'm glad you have a sense of humor," I said.

"Me, too."

Nate is a good-looking dude. He's tall and lanky. He has straight black hair that he's always brushing back from his forehead, round dark brown eyes, and an easy smile that makes a dimple appear on his right cheek.

"You're Lisa, right?" He studied me. "Saralynn told me about you. She didn't warn me you were dangerous."

I gave him a look. "Yes, I'm very dangerous." I guess that was my idea of flirting. I had pulled him to his feet. Now I realized I was still holding onto his arm. "How do you know Saralynn?"

He wiped more blood off his forehead with the sleeve of his black T-shirt. "We grew up near each other. On the same block."

"You're a senior, right?" I said. My phone beeped in my jeans pocket. A text. I ignored it.

He squinted at me. "How do you know that?"

I shrugged. "Saralynn might have mentioned it to me."

Saralynn and I are juniors. I hate that word, but it's awkward to say you're in eleventh grade. "You need to see the nurse," I said. "That cut on your forehead is kinda bad."

He nodded. "I didn't plan to give *blood* today." He said it like an old-time movie vampire.

I laughed. "You make a good vampire. Saralynn told me you're into scary movies and horror."

"Yeah, I collect posters and comics and masks and stuff," he said. "You seem to know a lot about me."

I shrugged again. I could feel my face growing hot. It was true. Saralynn and I did talk about him a lot. Ever since we watched him read a long Edgar Allan Poe poem at the senior talent show. I thought he was hot. Strange but hot.

I mean, Edgar Allan Poe? Seriously?

The bell rang. We were going to be late for fifth period.

I had a strong feeling about him. Like some kind of laser force field pulling me toward him. A hundred years ago, I think they called it love at first sight. Cornball music would be playing with lots of violins.

What I mean to say is that I liked the way he looked at me, and I liked talking to him. I even thought he looked cool with a line of blood leaking across his forehead.

"Nice bumping into you," I said.

He nodded. "Funny. Remind me to laugh."

Nate and I have been hanging out ever since. Sometimes it's just the two of us. Sometimes it was like the night of April 12, when we went to the hamburger hangout, Lefty's, with Saralynn and Nate's friend Isaac Brenner.

Yes, I remember the exact date. April 12. The night of the accident. The night of so much horror. The night I turned into an insane lunatic.

2.

"s that a real word?" Isaac asked. "Vomitorium?"

"Mr. Hammer explained it to us," Saralynn said. "In Drama class. They had these aisles in theaters. Like in Roman times. For the audience to leave the theater quickly. They were called vomitoriums. In Latin, it meant *spew forth*."

Isaac scratched his curly black hair. "You mean the audiences puked their guts out in the aisles?"

"No. That's a mistake people make," Saralynn told him. "Vomitoriums didn't have anything to do with vomiting."

I rolled my eyes. "Can we talk about something else? I mean, we came here to eat cheeseburgers, right? Why do we have to talk about vomitoriums?"

Nate nodded agreement. We were sitting in a wide, red vinyl booth in the back of the restaurant. He had his arm around my shoulders. Saralynn and Isaac sat facing us.

"'Cuz that's what the lunchroom looked like yesterday,"

7

Isaac said. "Kids were heaving all over the place. It was totally *sick*."

Nate's hand squeezed my shoulder. "Does anyone know what made those kids all toss their lunch?"

"Maybe the food?" Isaac said.

We laughed. Isaac is a total joker. He always knows the dumbest thing to say.

"It's still a mystery," Saralynn said. "Someone said they all had the mac and cheese. But what could go wrong with mac and cheese?"

Yesterday had been a bad day at school. A dozen kids had to be sent to the emergency room at Shadyside General. But this puke talk was making me queasy.

I was glad when the waitress came back to the booth to take our order. I recognized her from school. Rachel Martin. She is a senior, but we are in the same Politics and Government class.

"What's the special tonight?" Isaac asked her.

She blinked. "Cheeseburgers."

"That was the special last night," Isaac said.

Rachel poked him with the eraser on her pencil. "You're very sharp, Isaac."

"You shouldn't poke the customers," Isaac said, rubbing his shoulder. "Didn't Lefty tell you that?"

We all looked to the window that opened into the kitchen. We could see Lefty's back. He was at the grill, frying up cheeseburgers.

"Lefty said it was okay to poke you," Rachel said.

Isaac jumped up. "Really? I didn't know you liked me. Should we go to your place or mine?"

Saralynn pulled him back to the seat. "Ha ha. Funny."

"We'll have the usual," Nate told Rachel.

She scribbled something on her little pad. Then she poked Isaac again with the pencil, turned, and headed to the kitchen.

Nate slid his hand from behind my back. "Okay, phones on the table, guys." He slid his phone from his jeans pocket and set it down in the middle of the table.

The rest of us pulled out our phones and stacked them on top of Nate's in a neat pile.

"Hey, make sure Isaac didn't turn off his ringer," Saralynn said.

Nate pulled Isaac's phone from the pile and examined it.

"You guys really think I'd cheat?" Isaac asked, pretending to be hurt.

"Yes!" all three of us answered.

Nate moved the switch on Isaac's phone. He stared accusingly across the table. "You *did* have your ringer switched off."

Isaac raised his right hand. "Accident. I swear. Total accident."

This was a serious tradition we had. We piled the phones on the table. First phone to ring? The owner had to pay for dinner.

I was usually the loser. That's because my mom and dad

9

are total pests. They're your basic helicopter parents, hovering over me wherever I go. They call me constantly. They pretend they have a question they want to ask. But they're really just checking up on me.

When I don't pick up, they leave long voicemails. I mean, seriously. Who listens to *voicemails*?

At my old school I had a boyfriend they didn't like. Just because he was out of school and he had a tattoo sleeve on his right arm. He wasn't a bad guy, but they couldn't see beyond the tattoos.

I think he's the reason they don't trust me now.

Do they like Nate? I haven't asked them. I really don't care.

"What's up with your band?" Nate asked Isaac. Isaac has a rock band called The Black Holes. They say they are a Metallica cover band, but it's hard to tell when you listen to them.

Isaac had been shuffling the ketchup and mustard dispensers. Suddenly, he squeezed them at Nate. Nate dodged away. A spray of ketchup and mustard splashed the table.

"You really are a ten-year-old," Saralynn said, shaking her head.

"Sorry," Isaac said. "I didn't mean to squeeze them. Really. Thinking about my band gets me all tense." He grabbed some napkins and dabbed at the stains on the table.

"What's your problem?" Nate asked.

"We suck," Isaac said. He tugged at his thick mop of black hair. "We totally suck."

"Tell us something new," Saralynn said.

Isaac ignored her. "We have a gig Saturday night. At the Hothouse. You know. That club on Park almost to the River Road? And the dudes haven't learned any of the music. I can't even get them all to a rehearsal at the same time."

"We heard you at the senior talent show last month," Nate said. "You sucked *then*."

Isaac shook his head. "We've had a whole month to get even more sucky. It's a horror show, Nate. Seriously. You could put us in your horror collection. Right next to *Evil Dead II*."

Nate had at least two hundred horror films on DVD. Last weekend, he forced us all to watch *Evil Dead II*. It was his all-time favorite. Especially the flying eyeball scene.

Rachel brought us our cheeseburgers and fries. She started to set down the plates, then stopped. "Who spilled ketchup and mustard on the table?"

"Three guesses," Saralynn said.

Rachel stared at Isaac for a long moment. She laughed. Everyone likes Isaac. He's short and a little chubby, with a tangled nest of black hair and brown eyes that crinkle up when he smiles. Isaac is always making jokes and interrupting classes with his wisecracks. He says he has a desperate need for attention. I can't tell if that's another one of his jokes or not.

He's very smart. I don't think he studies very hard, but he's a straight-A student. And he learned to speak Mandarin. He says he wants to go to China for a year before he starts college.

Nate says Isaac wants to go to China just to get away from his band.

"Speaking of horror movies . . ." Saralynn started.

We were all into our cheeseburgers now. Lefty makes them juicy and piles on the lettuce and tomato and pickles.

"I have to do a video for Film class," Saralynn continued. "And I think we should do our own horror movie. Maybe in your attic, Nate. With all your totally gross horror masks?"

Nate swallowed a chunk of cheeseburger. He had juice running down his chin. I mopped it up with a paper napkin. "Sounds cool," he told Saralynn. "Do you have a script?"

"I have some ideas," she said. "But if we could use some of your props and masks and posters . . . it would be awesome."

"How about a vampire movie?" Isaac said. "My cousin works in a medical lab. I can probably get *buckets* of blood from him."

"I'm thinking something more sophisticated," Saralynn said. "Something paranormal."

"You'll still need blood," Isaac said.

Nate turned to me. "Lisa, you want to be in it?"

I shrugged. "Sure. Why not? But you know me. I'm not into horror. I mean, I really don't get it. What's the fun of being scared?"

Nate sighed. "You're hopeless."

"*Everyone* likes to be scared," Saralynn said. "It's like a basic human thing."

"Guess I'm not human," I said. "I always think horror movies are dumb."

Nate squeezed my arm. "I'll show you some movies that will change your mind."

"I'll tell you something scary," I said. "I sneaked out tonight. I'm not supposed to be here."

Saralynn set down her cheeseburger. "Lisa, you had to *sneak* out? It's Friday night. Why didn't your parents want you to go out?"

"Because they're jerks," I said. "I'm supposed to be in my room writing thank-you notes for my Sweet Sixteen party. Like that can't wait till tomorrow. I'm serious. My parents treat me like a total child."

Isaac pulled the pickles from his burger and jammed them into his mouth. "Wish *my* parents would treat me like a child," he muttered.

"What do you mean?" I said.

"They don't know I exist. No one ever says, 'Where are you going, Isaac?' Or 'What are you doing? What's up?' All they care about is their golf scores and their friends at the country club."

"You're lucky," I said. "My parents are always in my face."

I raised my eyes to the front of the restaurant and let out a startled cry. "See what I mean?"

3.

My dad stood just inside the door. He had his shiny blue hoodie open over a Cleveland Indians T-shirt. His wavy brown hair was unbrushed and stood up in tufts on his head. His eyes surveyed the restaurant until he found me. He stomped past some girls waiting for a table, making his way to our booth.

"Dad—what are you doing here?" My cry made some heads turn around.

My dad is tall and good-looking, with reddish brown hair and pale blue eyes in a tanned face. Mom says he looks like a young Clint Eastwood because of the lines down his cheeks and his hard expression.

I look more like my mother. Her parents came from Denmark. We're blonde and pale, tall and kind of bony.

Dad stopped a few feet from the booth. His hands were balled into fists at his sides. He's not violent at all. He does that when he's tense. He had bright red circles darkening his cheeks.

"Lisa, you promised to stay home," he said. He kept his blue eyes locked on me. I don't think he noticed that there were others at the table.

My heart started to pound in my chest. *Please don't embarrass me in front of my new friends.*

"Come on," Dad said, motioning for me to get up. "Mom and Morty are in the car."

I wanted to scream. But I forced my voice to stay low and steady. "I'll come home later, Dad."

He shook his head. "No. Now."

I pointed to my plate. "I haven't finished my cheeseburger."

"Hey, Mr. Brooks," Nate broke in. "I can drive Lisa home right after we eat."

Dad finally turned away from me. "Thanks, Nate. But we need Lisa to come home now." He raised his eyes to Saralynn and Isaac. "Sorry to interrupt your dinner."

He suddenly appeared embarrassed. As if he realized he'd gone too far. He's not a beast or anything. He's actually very reasonable most of the time.

I decided it would be easier to go with him rather than cause a big scene. I *did* sneak out of the house, after all. But I should be able to decide when I can go out with my friends. Like the thank-you cards couldn't wait a day or two?

Muttering under my breath, I squeezed past Nate and climbed out of the booth. I kept my eyes down and didn't look at my father.

"Do you have a jacket or something?" he asked. "It's pretty windy out."

"You're going to tell me how to dress now?" I snapped.

I waved goodbye to the others. They all flashed me sympathetic looks. They probably thought my dad was weird, following me to the restaurant.

I stormed angrily past him to the door and stepped outside. It was a blustery, cold night. It felt more like March than April. I was wearing a long-sleeved top over a short skirt and black tights. The wind brushed my hair straight back.

I spotted our Camry at the curb near the corner, ran to it, and dove into the backseat. As soon as I arrived, Morty started to wag his tail and pant like crazy. He bounced across the seat to me and began to give my face a ferocious tongue bath.

"Morty—down! Get off me!" I cried, laughing. My face is very ticklish. His tongue felt like sandpaper. "Stop! Morty! Give me a break!"

Morty is a big white sheepdog mix. My parents gave him to me for my birthday. He goes everywhere we go. He thinks he's a little puppy. He's always jumping on me and slobbering his tongue over my face.

I finally pushed him back. I wiped my cheeks with the sleeve of my top.

"I'm very disappointed in you," Mom said from the front passenger seat without turning around.

"It's not a big deal," I said. I could feel my anger grow. I had a heavy feeling in the pit of my stomach. Following me to Lefty's was a real invasion.

"I'm not eight years old," I said.

"Then don't act it." Mom still didn't turn around. She's very soft-spoken. And she doesn't like scenes.

I'm the one in the family with the hot temper.

Dad pulled the car away from the curb. He still hadn't said a word. He squealed into a turn onto Park Drive and headed for home. We live on the Village Road, about half a mile from the salon where Mom is a hairdresser.

"Slow down, Jimmy," Mom told him.

"Don't tell me how to drive," he snapped.

Now we were all snapping at each other. My fault, right?

I heard a pattering sound and saw that it had started to rain. Raindrops sparkled on the windshield in the light from an oncoming car.

"Slow down," Mom repeated, through gritted teeth. "The road is slippery."

"Lisa, we have to be able to trust you," Dad said.

"You *can* trust me," I said. "You had no right to—"

"How can we trust you when you lied to us and sneaked out of the house?" Dad said.

"I shouldn't have to sneak out," I told him. "Why did I sneak out? Because you're both impossible. You totally embarrassed me in front of my friends. Did you even think about that?"

"Jimmy, you went through a red light," Mom said. "Concentrate on your driving. We can have a family discussion when we get home."

"Oh, no," I groaned. "There won't be any family discussion. I—"

I stopped. And then I screamed: "Turn around! Turn around! I left my phone on the table." I pounded the back of Dad's seat. "Turn around!"

Dad spun the wheel. The car swerved.

Mom screamed.

Blinding yellow light blazed across the windshield.

I saw the sparkling raindrops. Like jewels in the bright light.

I felt a hard jolt. It tossed me forward, then back.

I felt the jolt and then heard the crash. An explosion of metal and glass.

In the bright light, I saw Dad's head snap forward. Saw his forehead slam into the steering wheel.

Still swerving. The car was still moving. The light seemed to be all around us, tossing us like on a bright ocean wave.

I saw Dad's head snap. And then I heard a *crack* and knew it was the crack of his skull. I knew it. Knew it.

I heard his skull crack, saw his face split open, saw dark blood rise up like a fountain and then pour down his forehead.

My head jerked to the side. The back door flew open. I heard a powerful rush of wind. I saw Morty leap out.

Morty, come back—

And then the pain hit me. The pain shot down the back

of my neck. The pain swept over me. My chest . . . my legs . . . my head. Blinding pain.

I'm blind. . . . No . . . I'm dead.

The bright light lifted. I sank . . . sank into a deep blackness.

4.

Then the light returned.

Pale, watery light with dark forms floating across it. Moving blurs. Like gazing into a camera totally out of focus.

I heard a murmur of voices, nearby but too soft to understand any words. I gazed up at the shifting light, struggling to squint away the gauzy curtain that kept me from seeing clearly.

As I blinked and squinted, the pain grew stronger. My head throbbed. I felt a painful throbbing at my temples. I tried to turn my head, but a sharp stab of pain forced me to stop.

"Should I increase it?" A woman's voice came from somewhere behind me. "It's already set near maximum."

It took me so long to realize I was in a bed.

On my back in a hospital bed.

The light billowed and pulsed and began to fade. The tide going out. Evening over the water.

I lay on the shore watching the sunset.

No. That was wrong. I wasn't thinking clearly.

I was on my back, staring up at the circles of light on the ceiling. Yes. I forced myself to focus.

And now I could see the thick orange tube stuck into my wrist. And a narrow window with the blinds half-drawn. My hands at my sides on the white linen sheet.

Ignoring the pain, I turned my head and saw a bed across from me. I gasped as my dad came into focus. Yes. I remembered the accident now. The crash and the shatter of metal and glass and the hard jolt of the collision.

I remembered the accident. And now I stared at my dad in the bed across from me. He went in and out of focus, clear and then a blur. His head—it was slumped forward. Bright red blood poured down his face.

And the steering wheel—

—*The shaft of the steering wheel was jammed into his forehead.*

The steering wheel poked out of his head. The blood flowed all around it and puddled on the floor.

He didn't move. He just slumped forward on the bed, with the blood-spattered steering wheel stuck deep in his head.

Where were the nurses? Where were the doctors?

I turned away. I couldn't bear to watch. And I opened my mouth in a shrill wail of horror. "Help him! Somebody help him!"

5.

My shrill screams made my throat hurt. The room spun crazily around me.

My mother's face slid into view above me. She appeared even paler than usual, as if her skin was white paper tight against her cheeks.

"Mom?"

She blinked several times. I saw tears form in her eyes. "Lisa? You're awake? Oh, thank goodness!"

Lifting my head, I saw a gray-haired man in a green lab coat step up behind her. He had a clipboard in one hand. A stethoscope swung on his chest as he moved.

"Dad!" I screamed. "Take care of Dad!"

Neither of them turned around. They narrowed their eyes at me.

I turned my gaze to the bed across from me. "Dad?"

The bed was empty.

Mom placed a hand on my shoulder. "Lisa, why were

you screaming?" I saw that her other arm was in a cast inside a blue sling.

"I-I thought I saw Dad," I stammered. Again, the room started to spin. "In that bed. I saw him so clearly. He was bleeding. I mean, his head was down and blood was pouring . . . and no one was helping him. No one."

The gray-haired man edged my mother to the side. He peered down at me with silvery eyes behind black-framed glasses. He had thick, arched eyebrows that looked like fat white caterpillars. "I'm Dr. Martino," he said. "Lisa, I'm glad you've come around so quickly. You've been out since last night."

"I've been out?" I glanced at the window. Orange sunlight filled the bottom half. Afternoon sunlight?

"You've had a serious concussion," Dr. Martino said. His breath smelled of coffee. Light reflected on his glasses and hid his eyes. "You may have nightmares and even hallucinations for a while. Your brain had a nasty jolt."

I shut my eyes. Everything hurt. My whole body. Even my eyelids.

"Hallucinations?" I said. I opened my eyes. "You mean just now when I saw my dad in the bed?"

The doctor nodded. Beside him, Mom let out a sob. She cut it off quickly. She never likes to show emotion. It's a Scandinavian thing, I think.

"I really thought I saw him," I said, my throat suddenly tight. "I can't believe I was hallucinating."

"We will have to keep you here," Dr. Martino said. "Perhaps for a week or more. Internal bleeding is something we have to watch for. We need to keep a close watch for that. You may suffer other hallucinations. I feel I must warn you."

I only half-heard his words. He kept fading in and out. His eyebrows seemed to move on their own as if they were alive.

I twisted my head toward Mom. "But—Dad? Where is Dad? Is he okay?"

Mom bit her bottom lip. She took a breath before she replied. "No, Lisa. I'm sorry," she whispered. "He . . . he's not okay."

PART
TWO

6.

I don't want to describe my week in the hospital. It was a time of boredom and headaches and frustration and pain and tears and bad dreams. The first time I was allowed to walk on my own to the bathroom across the hall, I suddenly saw the floor turn to a swampy green ooze. I felt the sticky-wet gunk on the bottoms of my paper hospital slippers and watched in horror as the hot ooze bubbled quickly up to my ankles.

I began hopping up and down, frantically trying to scrape the green slime off my feet. "It won't come off! It won't come off!" I screamed.

I had to be rescued by two nurses, who held me firmly by the elbows and returned me shaking and shuddering to my bed.

"Am I always going to be crazy?" I asked one of them, a tall black woman who was strong enough to lift me off my feet and onto the bed.

"We're *all* a little crazy," she said. She had a surprisingly high, soft voice. "You're going to be fine. Give it time."

I wasn't sure I believed her.

I had nothing but time in the hospital, time to stare up at the ceiling and think about my dad. Mom rented me a television over my bed. But the only time I turned it on, it was a commercial for dog food. I started to sob because Morty ran from the car and hadn't been seen since. I switched the TV off and never turned it on again.

Some people sent sympathy cards and some sent get-well cards. My cousins in Vermont sent a huge bouquet of white and yellow lilies. The sharp fragrance of the flowers filled the room, and I started to sneeze. I'm allergic to lilies, I guess. The flowers had to go.

Who cares anyway?

I had a lot of bitter thoughts and a lot of thoughts I couldn't describe. I guess you'd call them dark.

When I finally was released and sitting in the backseat of an unfamiliar car with Mom at the wheel, everything appeared too bright. I kept my head down, waiting for my eyes to adjust. But they refused, and everything I saw had a blinding glare around it.

"Mom, how can you drive with one hand?" My voice was hoarse, I guess because I hadn't used it much. I rubbed my right wrist. It ached from where the tube had been inserted. I had a round blue bruise there.

She didn't answer.

I shielded my eyes with one hand. The sunlight was just

too bright for me. I wondered if sunglasses would help. We pulled out of the hospital parking lot and a few seconds later were speeding through the narrow streets of the Old Village.

I should have felt happy. Freedom at last! I was going home. But it was like happy feelings took too much energy. I slumped against the seatback. I felt numb. You know when your foot falls asleep? That's how my whole *self* felt.

"Mom, are you okay?"

Still shielding my eyes, I peered out the windshield— and let out a sharp cry as I saw the big, white dog slowly crossing the street. "Mom—stop! Stop the car! Look—it's Morty."

The car didn't slow down. Mom swerved the wheel to the left.

"No—Mom! You're going to hit him! Mom—stop! *Please!*"

She jammed her foot on the gas. The car roared forward. I saw the oncoming car. A dark blue SUV with a chrome grille that looked like animal teeth. I heard its horn blare like a siren.

And then the crash tossed me hard against the back of the front seat.

Oh, no! Nooooo! Not again!

I bounced back against my seat. I saw Mom's head hit the steering wheel. It didn't bounce up. It stayed down on the wheel, her arms limp at her sides.

A gusher of blood from Mom's head splashed onto the

windshield. The windshield was quickly splattered bright red.

Not again. Not again.

The car began moving again. Slumped over the wheel, Mom didn't budge. But the car began roaring forward. I couldn't see out, couldn't see through the covering of darkening blood over the windshield.

I reached over the seat and grabbed Mom by the shoulders and shook her, shook her hard. "Wake up! Please! Stop the car! You've *got* to stop the car."

And then her head slowly turned to me. And I saw that it wasn't Mom. It was my dad, smiling so sweetly at me, Dad with his head split wide open, smiling at me from beyond the grave.

7.

Ifelt a hard tug and opened my eyes to find Mom shaking me by the shoulders. "Wake up, Lisa. Come on. Wake up." Her voice was a tense whisper.

I saw the curtains blowing at my bedroom window. Darkness behind them. Still night.

I blinked several times, trying to force away the sight of my dad's split head.

"Another nightmare," Mom said, shaking her head. Her blonde hair was matted against one side of her face. She straightened her long nightshirt. Her hands stayed on my shoulders, soothing them now.

I tried to say something, but my throat was still clogged with sleep.

Mom clicked on the blue lamp on my bedside table. I turned away from the sudden bright light. "You've been home a week, and you're still having the nightmares," she said. "When do you see your doctor next?"

"Dr. Shein? Not sure," I managed to whisper. I ran both

hands back through my hair. My skin was damp from perspiration. "The same nightmare," I told her. "I was in the car, and I saw Dad again."

Mom sighed. In the harsh light from my lamp, she suddenly looked a lot older. "Dr. Shein says it will take time, Lisa."

"But I'm not getting better, Mom. I keep seeing Dad and Morty everywhere." I pulled myself to a sitting position. My sheets were damp, too, from sweat. I shuddered. "Nightmares and hallucinations. I'm a total crazy person."

"You know that's not true. You know this is only temporary. I'm sure that as time passes—"

"Mom, I really think it will help me if I go back to school."

Mom sighed again. "It's four in the morning. I know you've just had a frightening night. Do you really want to have this discussion now?"

"I don't want a discussion at all," I said. "I just want to go back to school. I . . . I haven't seen any of my friends. And all because you say I'm not ready."

"It's not me," Mom snapped. "It's Dr. Shein. She's the trained psychiatrist. She's been working with you since the hospital."

"But, Mom—"

"I think we should listen to her advice, don't you? I know how frustrated you are. But she feels you have to work out some of your grief, some of your guilty feelings before you can go back to your normal life."

"Wow. That's a mouthful, Mom. Have you been practicing that answer all day?"

She took a step back. I could see that I'd hurt her. I didn't really mean to sound that angry and sarcastic. *Where did that come from?*

Maybe Dr. Shein was right. Maybe I wasn't fit to see other people yet.

I'm going to rely on her, I decided. *She's been so wonderful to talk to. I'll do whatever she thinks best.*

"Sorry, Mom," I blurted out quickly. "I didn't mean—"

"Let's try to get back to sleep," she said.

The next day was a cloudy, gray Saturday, gathering storm clouds low in the sky. Outside our front window, the whole world appeared in somber shades of gray, which fit my mood perfectly.

At breakfast, Mom said it was okay for Nate to come over, and he showed up a little after eleven. I greeted him with an awkward hug. I could see he was nervous.

"Hey," he said. "You look good."

"Liar." I had circles around my eyes from so little sleep. And I'd lost at least ten pounds. I just didn't have any appetite.

We sat down on the low green leather armchairs across from one another in the den. He kept gazing at me, studying me as if he'd never seen me before. And his right leg kept tapping up and down, like he was really tense.

We'd been texting and we did some video chats, but it

was different being in the same room with him. Sure, I was happy to see him. But it was hard to get a conversation started. I felt like someone had built a tall picket fence between us, and we were trying to talk over the fence.

"Sorry about your dad," Nate said, lowering his eyes to the white carpet.

I should have just said *thank you* or nodded and kept silent. But I felt a burst of anger. "I can't talk about it," I said, my voice cracking. "My dad is dead, and it's all my fault."

Nate actually flinched. As if I'd hit him.

"Sorry," I muttered. "Sorry. Sorry. Sorry."

"It isn't true," he said finally. "It wasn't your fault, Lisa. He was driving—not you. *He* caused the accident. You can't blame yourself."

"Ha," I said bitterly.

The phone rang. I heard Mom hurry to answer it in the kitchen.

I stood up and climbed onto Nate's lap. I thought maybe if he held me for a while I could lift myself from this dark mood.

Nate put his arms around me. I snuggled my face against his cheek. I could hear Mom talking on the phone.

"Every time it rings, I think it's someone calling to say they found Morty," I told Nate. I sighed. "My poor dog. He ran out of the car and just kept running. He was so scared. And now it'd been nearly two weeks. . . . "

Nate tightened his arms around me. "He'll turn up, Lisa."

I shoved his arms away and jumped to my feet. "Give

me a break!" I cried. "Stop being so cheerful. What's your problem, anyway? Can't you see that my life is *over?*"

His mouth dropped open.

I shook both fists at my sides. "I *killed* my father, Nate. How can I live with that?"

He stared up at me from the chair. I could see his eyes dart from side to side. He was thinking hard. He didn't know how to deal with me.

Who would? I knew I was being impossible but I couldn't stop myself.

He lowered his hands to the arms of the chair. I think he wanted to get up. He wanted to leave.

But the front doorbell rang, startling us both. And I heard a dog bark outside.

"Nate—it's Morty!" I cried. I tugged Nate to his feet. "Someone has found Morty!"

We both tore across the living room to the front door. I pulled the door open and held my arms out to hug my dog.

8.

The young guy on the front stoop wore a black leather vest over a white T-shirt and baggy denim jeans. He had a green and yellow John Deere cap pulled over his forehead. A stubble of black beard covered his tanned cheeks.

"I saw your thing online about your missing dog," he said. "I found him in my backyard and—"

"But that's not my dog!" I cried. "That's not Morty!"

My voice came out high and shrill. Nate put a hand on my shoulder as if to steady me.

"Wrong dog," he told the guy.

The dog gazed up at me, panting softly. It was some kind of shepherd-mix. Its tail was tucked between its hind legs. A patch of gray fur on its back was missing.

The guy squinted at me, then at the dog. "You sure?"

"Of *course* I'm sure," I snapped. I wanted to slam the door shut. I didn't want to look at that ragged, forlorn animal on my stoop. I wanted Morty.

"Who is it, dear?" Mom called from inside the house.

"No one," I shouted back.

"Sorry," the guy said. "I thought maybe—"

"Thanks for trying," Nate told him.

I pushed the door shut. I led the way back to the den. I was walking stiffly, as if every muscle in my body had tightened. Total tension and frustration and disappointment.

Through the living room window, I saw the guy leading the dog down the driveway. He and the dog had their heads lowered with the same unhappy expression on their faces. It would have made a funny photo . . . if I was in the mood for funny.

In the den, Nate slid his arms around my waist. His hair fell over his forehead as he started to kiss me. I cut the kiss off with a shudder. I shook my head. "I'm sorry, Nate. I'm just not good company right now. Seriously. You'd better go."

Late that night I sat straight up in bed when I heard a dog howling outside my bedroom window. I was still in that space between asleep and awake, but I knew I wasn't dreaming.

The window stood half-open. The curtains at the window were still. No breeze tonight. But as I climbed to my feet, I could see pale lights, the sky clear and full of stars.

I tugged my sneakers on without lacing them. And found my jean jacket in my closet. As I pulled it over my shoulders, I heard the dog howl again. A long, mournful sound.

"Morty. I'm coming, Morty."

I crept downstairs. The steps creaked beneath my feet. The house was dark. It smelled of popcorn, the late-night snack Mom and I shared while watching a dumb comedy movie on TV.

Moving silently, I made my way out the back door, across the dew-wet back lawn, and into the woods that stretched behind our house.

The dog howled again. Close by. Very close.

My heart started to pound.

A brilliant full moon shone down through the trees. The sky was so clear tonight. Above the spring-bare tree limbs I could see the stars high above me.

The moonlight . . . the starlight . . . made the whole world glow like silver. Unreal.

The cool air made my skin tingle. I pulled the jean jacket tighter. I listened hard. "Morty, where are you? Morty— I'm coming."

Another howl. And then a tall shadow moved between the silvery trees. A shadow. A figure. Running fast.

It burst into view, and I tried to scream.

I was staring at some kind of *creature*.

I grabbed a tree trunk and wrapped my arms around it, as if to hold myself up. I stared into the silvery light and watched the *thing* trot through the trees.

He stood on two legs and ran upright, like a human. But he was bare-chested, and even in this strange light, I could see that his body was weird, huge, long-fingered hands at the end of skinny arms, a nearly bald head, red glowing eyes. He stopped for a moment in a pool of light. And I saw his face . . . distorted . . . features twisted. . . . Not a human face.

His ears stuck straight up, like pig's ears. A long animal snout poked from between his cheeks. His snout hung open. I could see two rows of long, fanglike teeth.

And suddenly, with my arms wrapped tightly around the cold, rough tree trunk, I knew I was dreaming again. Another nightmare. You know how when you are asleep and you are totally aware that you are in a dream.

Wake up. Wake up, Lisa.

Why couldn't I wake myself from this one?

The creature made ugly growling sounds. He was a blur as he moved toward me. And then he was only a shadow again, a shadow with glowing ruby eyes. He seemed to melt into the darkness.

Was he really there at all?

Wake up, Lisa. Hurry. Wake up from this nightmare.

But there was no escape this time. I heard a groan. And then the shadow swept over me, grabbed me, shook me hard, grunting my name.

9.

et me go!" I shrieked. My eyes were shut tight. "Get
off me!"

"Lisa, what are you doing out here?"

I opened my eyes to see my mother, hair wild about her
face, a raincoat pulled over her nightshirt. Her eyes were
wide with fright. They reflected the eerie light from the
moon. Her chin trembled. She was shivering.

"What are you doing out here? Why are you in the woods
in the middle of the night? I was frantic. I searched everywhere for you."

I leaned forward and forced her to hug me. I just stood
there leaning into her, wrapped up in her, my head pressed
against the front of her coat.

"Lisa? Can you talk? Are you okay?" Her voice trembled on the night air.

I stood up. Her warmth lingered on my skin. "I
thought . . . I thought I was dreaming. I saw a creature. An

ugly half-human creature that ran into the shadows, Mom. I saw it and I knew I had to be dreaming."

Mom had tears in her eyes. They glistened in the moon-light like twin pearls. "But you're not dreaming, Lisa. Look where you are. You're in the woods."

I gazed around. The cool night air made me shiver. I hugged myself to stop my shakes. "Was I *sleepwalking*?"

Mom hesitated. "I guess you were."

"Something new," I said, rolling my eyes. "The night-mares weren't bad enough. Now I have to go roaming around like a lunatic in the woods." I sighed. "At least I was sane enough to put on clothes. I'm not walking around out here totally naked. That's a good sign, right?"

I was trying to get a smile from my mom. I didn't like to see tears in her eyes. She wasn't an emotional person. She wasn't supposed to cry.

She didn't smile and she didn't answer my question. Without another word, I took her arm and we began to walk to the house. After a few steps, I stopped.

She stumbled but caught her balance. "Lisa? What's wrong?"

"What about the creature?" I asked. "Was he real, too?"

"Of course not," she said softly.

"But what does that mean? That I was sleepwalking and having a nightmare at the same time?" I sighed. "Will I always be this crazy, Mom?"

"You're not crazy." Her voice was a whisper. "Don't say that."

"Well, will I ever be normal again? Will I?"

She stepped into shadows. I couldn't see her face. I couldn't hear her whispered reply. My question lingered in the air like a forgotten whisper.

The next morning I slept in and woke up refreshed. I thought about the day. I remembered I had an appointment with Dr. Shein. Before that, I wanted to walk over to Nate's house and apologize for how badly I treated him the day before.

Of course, Mom thought it might be too much for me. "Why don't you invite him over here?"

"Mom," I said, "I can walk three blocks in broad daylight. Seriously. You have to let me try to do normal things. It's the only way I'll ever return to a normal life."

I didn't shout and I didn't plead. I kept my voice low and steady, and I think my argument won her over.

"Maybe you're right. Walk to Nate's. Go ahead. Get out of the house for a couple of hours. I don't want to hold you back. Let's see how you do."

A couple of hours? She was treating me like a mental patient. But so what? I got my way. I texted Nate and told him I was coming over.

It was a warm spring afternoon. I pulled a blue, long-sleeved top over a pair of denim shorts. "You need a jacket," Mom called from the kitchen.

"No, I don't," I shouted.

"Don't forget your appointment with Dr. Shein," she yelled.

"I won't forget." I stepped outside, squinting into the sunlight, and took a deep breath. The air smelled so fresh and sweet.

Across the street, the dogwood trees in the Millers' front yard were just beginning to show their white blossoms. Two little boys in their driveway were tossing a Nerf baseball back and forth. They waved to me as I walked to the sidewalk.

Our front lawn needed to be mowed. It was overgrown with weeds, and the brown fall leaves hadn't been raked. Dad had always taken care of the lawn. Mom probably hadn't given it a thought.

I crossed Pines Road. An SUV filled with kids in soccer uniforms rumbled past. The houses on this block were big, with wide sloping lawns. I saw two robins fighting over a fat brown earthworm, a real tug-of-war.

A beautiful spring day and I was enjoying my walk, feeling like a human again, feeling like I could face the world and move on. Just move on.

The walk was refreshing and enjoyable—until I arrived at Nate's house. And then I was heaved back . . . back into a world of horror.

10.

Nate lives in a long, ranch-style house, dark redwood with purple shutters beside the windows. The purple shutters were his dad's idea. His dad is kind of an old-style hippie. He tries to be very cool. He sells life insurance, but he's also a jazz musician and a painter.

Nate's mom is tall and thin and very pretty in an old-fashioned TV sitcom way. She likes to chatter and gossip. She is the nicest person in the world. Nate has a younger brother, Tim, who looks like a Nate clone, but I don't know him very well.

Actually, the whole family could be clones. They are all lanky and tall with straight black hair and dark eyes.

I walked up Nate's driveway. His dad's red Prius was parked at the top of the driveway. The sun was reflected in their living room window making it glow like gold. I turned toward the front stoop but stopped when I heard voices. From the backyard?

Yes. I made my way around the side of the garage,

stepping over a coiled green garden hose. I smelled something sweet from the open kitchen window. Mrs. Goodman is an awesome baker.

Nate's backyard is fenced in by tall, straight evergreen shrubs. I saw a row of shrubs, gleaming in the sunlight. And then I heard a scream.

I stepped past the garage onto the back lawn. And cried out as I saw a hideous green creature. A demon. From out of my nightmares. Only this one was real, as real as the grass and the blue sky and the gray squirrel that leaped out of its way and darted from the yard.

The green creature dove out of the shadows of the tall shrubs and scrambled across the yard. I saw Saralynn with her back turned.

No time to warn her. I tried to scream but I couldn't make a sound.

No time. No time.

The creature looked like something out of a horror movie with huge, three-fingered hands, a round green head with rows of long pointed teeth hanging from its mouth, a slender green body, naked, totally naked.

A few feet from Saralynn, it turned. It *saw* me! It spun away from her and came galloping at me, grunting, its huge bare feet thundering over the grass.

Before I could move, it dove forward—and grabbed me around the waist.

I opened my mouth and uttered a shrill scream.

11.

"You idiot!" I cried. "You stupid idiot!"

Nate laughed and slid the green creature mask off his head. His dark hair was damp and matted across his forehead. "Lisa? Did I scare you?"

I pumped both fists against his green rubber chest. "How could you *do* that to me? Did you think that was *funny*?"

"Oops. Sorry," he said, his smile fading. "I just wasn't thinking. I'm sorry."

"You ruined the whole scene," I heard a voice behind me say. I turned and saw Isaac with a little camcorder in his hand. "We'll have to start again."

"Too bad," I said. "I can't believe you would do that to me, Nate. Especially after . . . after . . ."

He tried to slide his green arm around my shoulders but I backed away. "I just got carried away," he said. "Guess I *like* being a demon too much."

"We're sorry," Saralynn said, her eyes on Nate. "It's just that we've been working for days on my horror video."

"Do you like the demon costume?" Nate said, thumping the green chest with one fist. "It was actually used in an old Universal horror film back in the fifties. It's from my costume collection."

"Hey, Nate, you should do it *without* the mask," Isaac said. "Your face is a lot scarier."

Saralynn put an arm around my waist. "Lisa, forgive us. Sometimes Nate is an idiot."

"You don't understand," I said. "These days, I'm scared of my own reflection. Last night I saw a creature running through the woods. And now—now when I saw you in your costume coming at me . . ." My voice trailed off.

Saralynn kept her arm around my waist. "We know you've been having a tough time."

I took a deep breath and forced myself to stop trembling. "I'm going to stop being ridiculous," I said. "I promise. I'm going to be myself again. You'll see."

"Maybe we should go inside," Nate said.

"We need to shoot the rest at night," Isaac said. "It's too nice outside to be scary."

I started to follow them to the house. I felt much better. They really were good friends. Other kids might have laughed or made jokes or tried to embarrass me for seeing a demon in the backyard. But they tried to assure me that I wasn't crazy.

Nate stepped up beside me as we made our way along the side of the garage. "I have a new horror film on DVD," he said. "*My Big Fat Blood-Soaked Wedding*. Have you seen it?"

"Of course not," I said.

"I heard it's a riot," Isaac said.

"Let's watch it," Saralynn said. "Nate, what have you got for snacks?"

I stopped at the kitchen door. Through the window, I could see Nate's mom taking something out of the oven. The smell of chocolate floated over the backyard. "I can't stay," I said.

"Sorry," Nate said, squeezing my hand. "A horror film is probably a bad idea. I didn't think."

"It's not that," I said. "I have a doctor appointment. I just came over to apologize. You know. For yesterday when you came over. I was a beast. I'm really sorry. I—"

"Has the doctor been helpful?" Saralynn asked.

"She's wonderful," I said. "She's so supportive. She makes me feel I really can get over this."

"That's so nice you have someone good to talk to," Saralynn said.

Behind her, Isaac was waving frantically, trying to get my attention. I turned to him. "What's up?"

"Hey, I have a great idea," he said. "Why don't you come hear my band at the Hothouse Friday night? We totally suck, but maybe it will take your mind off everything."

"Yeah. Maybe," I said.

But I realized I didn't want to do that. Since the accident, I'd only seen my three friends. I hadn't seen anyone else from school.

And if I went to hear Isaac's band, all these people would

be feeling sorry for me, and staring at me, and giving me sympathetic looks, and offering me condolences and saying how sorry they were.

I knew they'd all mean well. But I couldn't take it. I knew all that attention and all that sympathy would freak me out.

"So you'll come?" Isaac said.

"Well . . . I'll ask Dr. Shein if it's a good idea," I said.

Nate tugged at the neck of his green rubber costume. "I've got to get out of this thing," he groaned. "It's two hundred degrees in here."

I gazed at the demon mask crumpled in his hand. "You make a terrifying monster," I said.

For some reason, Nate blushed. Then he grinned at me. "Seriously. That's my real personality." His cheeks remained red.

I saw Saralynn flash him a disapproving look. Like he shouldn't have made that joke.

What's going on with those two? I wondered. *Is there something I'm not getting? Are they more than friends?*

12.

Dr. Shein has one weird habit that I've noticed. She has a white mug filled with yellow pencils on her desk beside the phone. And as we talk, she chews on an eraser. By the time our session is over, she has completely chewed the eraser off. I've never seen her spit one out. I think she swallows them.

Weird, right?

Just a nervous habit, I guess. Aside from the eraser-chewing, she is totally normal and nice and just an awesome, sweet, understanding person. I couldn't have survived all that has happened to me without her, and that's the truth.

Now I sat in the red leather armchair across from her wide glass desk. My hands were sweaty and left a trail of dampness on the chair arms. I kept crossing and uncrossing my legs.

Yes, Dr. Shein was always understanding and never judgmental. But it made me tense whenever I told her about the crazy things I had imagined or done. I was eager for her to think that I was getting better, even if I didn't believe it myself.

The sun had come out early in the afternoon and filled the windows behind her with yellow light. Her short blonde hair appeared to glow. She has bright blue eyes behind her frameless glasses and a friendly expression, even though she seldom smiles.

She leaned forward as we talked, her eyes on me, her hands clasped over the glass desktop. Her desk was empty except for a red phone, a small silver clock, a framed photo of a yellow Lab, and the notepad on which she scribbled notes.

"Go on, Lisa. Tell me what happened the other night," she said. She has a soft voice just above a whisper. Sometimes I have to lean forward in the chair to hear her. "You seem reluctant to talk today. Is anything special troubling you?"

"Not really," I said. I gazed at the large painting of a beach and ocean waves on the wall at her side. "I mean, nothing special. Just . . ."

She rolled the pencil in her fingers. "Just . . . what?"

"Well, I think I went sleepwalking," I started. "I was dreaming, I guess. A sound woke me up. Animal cries. And I woke up in the woods."

I swallowed.

"You sleepwalked into the woods?" she asked.

"My mother found me and shook me awake," I answered. "But before she did, I saw something frightening. A creature. Half-human, half . . . creature. Very weird and ugly."

"How clearly did you see it?" she asked softly. "Did you run? Did it follow you?"

"N-no. It disappeared into the trees." My voice broke. "Am I going totally crazy? How can I be seeing these things? I never sleepwalked before. I mean . . . does this mean I'm getting *worse*?"

She set down the pencil and motioned to the bottle of water in my lap. "Take some water, Lisa. You're upsetting yourself. We've talked about this process before."

"I know, but—"

She swept back her hair with one hand. "You're not getting worse. As we've said, getting better is a process. But the first thing you always need to remember is that you are going to get better. You are going to get okay again, and all of these symptoms will disappear."

I could hear her speaking, but I couldn't concentrate on what she was saying. I was picturing the shadowy creature in the woods. My whole body shuddered, suddenly feeling the damp cold of the woods all over again.

"I understand about imagining that I see Morty," I said, "and about thinking I see my dad. We've already talked about my guilty feelings and how they keep appearing. But, Dr. Shein, why did I see some kind of demon?"

"Maybe your demons have to come out," she replied. She tapped both hands on the glass desktop. "Lisa, your symptoms are *not* unusual for someone who has had the kind of traumatic accident you have."

"But how do we make them stop?" My voice came out

high and shrill. The water bottle rolled out of my lap, and I bent over to retrieve it on the dark carpet.

"By talking," she said. "You and I will keep talking, and you will see improvement every week. I promise."

"I like talking to you," I blurted out. "I mean . . . you've made me feel better already."

That made her smile. She scribbled some words rapidly on the yellow notepad in front of her.

"I have a couple of suggestions to help things along," she said. She twisted the slender gold watch on her wrist. "First of all, go back to school on Monday."

"Really?" I cried. I felt a burst of happiness.

She nodded. "It will be good for you to be back with your friends in a normal setting. And schoolwork will help take your mind off your troubled feelings."

"Oh, thank you," I said. "I've been wanting to go back. But my mom—"

"I also think you need something else to occupy your mind," she continued.

I squinted at her. "I don't understand. Do you mean like a hobby? Or an after-school job maybe?"

She tapped the pencil eraser against her lips. "Do you think you're ready for an after-school job?"

I shrugged. "I think so. And we could use the money since Mom can't go back to work."

"What kind of job, Lisa? Did you do any kind of work back in Shaker Heights?"

"Well . . ." I thought hard. "Not really. I didn't have a job. But . . . I did do a lot of babysitting."

Behind her eyeglasses, her eyes grew wide. "Babysitting? Really?"

"Yes," I said. "I'm good with kids. And I like taking care of them. I took care of my cousin Steven . . . until his family moved to Santa Barbara."

Dr. Shein nodded. "That might not be a bad idea. Perhaps caring for someone else will help you pull your mind from your own problems."

She pulled open a file drawer under her desk. "You know what? Now that you mention it, I might have something for you."

I leaned forward in my chair. "A babysitting job?"

She sifted through some folders and pulled out a sheet of paper. "Yes. Here it is. I'd almost forgotten. I know someone who is looking for a babysitter for her little boy. She worked at the hospital where I trained."

"Wow. That's wonderful," I said.

Her eyes scanned the page, then returned to me. "Her name is Brenda Hart. Her little boy is eight, I think."

"Awesome," I said. "This is so totally nice of you."

She copied down the information on her yellow pad, tore off the sheet, and handed it to me.

"Thank you, Dr. Shein," I said. I glanced at the name and address. My eyes stayed on the address. "They live on Fear Street?"

"Yes, they do," she replied. "You don't have a problem with Fear Street, do you, Lisa?"

I hesitated. "Well . . ."

"Surely, you don't believe all the foolish scary stories about that street. The ancient curses everyone talks about. You don't believe in such a thing as an evil street—do you?"

I blinked. "No. Of course not."

PART
THREE

13.

"You're new in town," Isaac said. "You don't understand about Fear Street."

"Please don't try to discourage me," I told him. "I really need this job. Mom can't go back to the salon because of her broken arm. And I'm really good at babysitting."

He put a hand on my arm. "Lisa, you should think about this. Seriously."

It was after school on Monday. My first day back was a nonevent. I expected kids to make a big fuss and tell me how sorry they were about my dad and about the accident.

But no one said much of anything. In fact, most people in my classes acted as if I'd never been away. That was a total relief, believe me.

Saralynn was really nice. She helped me bring my science notebook up to date in study hall. And she gave me some other worksheets and test-prep papers I was missing.

Nate was very kind, too. I told him I wanted to walk to Isaac's house after school and watch his band rehearse. He said he'd pick me up there and drive me to my job interview on Fear Street.

It was a warm spring day. Red and yellow tulips bobbed in the flower beds in front of Isaac's house. Leaves on the trees had started to open, revealing the bright, fresh green color you only see in early spring.

Isaac's band practiced in the garage behind his house. I could hear them as I walked up his gravel driveway. And I could tell they were *terrible* from halfway up the drive.

Isaac has three little sisters, and I could see them watching me from an open window at the side of the house. All three of them had their hands over their ears.

The garage door was open. I saw Isaac, knees bent, swaying from side to side as he played lead guitar. He nodded as I approached. Two other guys were behind him, deeper in the garage. I saw Booker Todd, a guy I knew from school, playing a left-handed bass guitar. And a short, skinny kid I didn't recognize, who looked about twelve, banging away on part of a drum set.

I honestly couldn't tell if they were playing the same song or three different songs. Maybe it was supposed to be like jazz where the musicians all go off in different directions.

I stood in the driveway watching them, keeping a forced smile on my face so they'd think I was enjoying it. Inside the house, I could hear the three sisters arguing loudly about something.

Finally, Isaac ended the number. He slid the guitar over

his head and set it down on the garage floor. "Hey, Lisa." He walked over to me, scratching his curly black hair. He had a big sweat stain on the front of his Vampire Weekend T-shirt. Behind him in the garage, the two other guys had water bottles tilted to their mouths.

"I know we suck," Isaac said in a hushed voice, glancing back at the two players. "You don't have to pretend."

"You only have three guys in your band?" I asked.

He wiped sweat off his forehead with a T-shirt sleeve. "No. Derek Palmer plays saxophone. But his parents grounded him for a week because he got wasted at Kerry Reacher's party last Friday and threw up on the living room couch after he got home."

"Not cool," I said.

"Not cool. And that kid—" Isaac pointed. "He's not the real drummer. He lives across the street. He's totally clueless. Jamie Weiner says he's quitting because we're hopeless."

"Bad attitude," I said.

He smiled. "Hey, not a bad name for a band."

I heard a car rumble by and thought it was Nate. "Nate's picking me up for my job interview," I said, glancing to the street.

"Yeah, I know. On Fear Street," Isaac said. "You'll see. It looks like a normal street. Normal houses. Normal people. But it's not normal . . . not at all."

"Please—" I started, raising a hand to silence him.

"Listen to me, Lisa. There's a real curse on the street. It's not a joke. It's not made up. They teach us about Fear Street and the Fear family in school. Seriously."

I shook my head. "Every town has its legends," I said. "Every town has its spooky stories. Even Shaker Heights had houses people said were haunted. And—"

"There were two families who hated each other," Isaac continued. "The Goodes and the Fears. They put curses on each other. They practiced dark magic and sorcery. They teach us all this in history class in sixth grade."

He placed his hands on my shoulders. "I can see you don't believe me. But there have been horrible murders on Fear Street, Lisa. People with their heads missing and their blood drained and—"

"Stop!" I cried. "I really don't believe this horror-movie stuff, Isaac. Stop trying to scare me."

He held onto my shoulders. To my surprise, his expression changed. His eyes went wide. He pulled me close, lowered his face to mine, and kissed me. It was a fierce, needy kiss. His lips felt dry and rough.

I was so startled, I didn't pull back. I just stood there and let him kiss me. His hold on my shoulders kept me in place. I couldn't breathe.

I was just so surprised.

But then I turned my face away and stumbled out of his grasp. "No, Isaac," I managed to choke out. "Please. You know that Nate and I—"

I gasped as I realized I was staring at Nate. He stood a few feet down the driveway.

Did he see us kiss?

The red afternoon sun beamed down on him, like catching him in a spotlight of fire. He had the strangest expression on his face, his eyes locked coldly on Isaac.

14.

"How's band practice?" Nate finally said to Isaac.

Isaac's face was bright red. He shrugged. "You know."

I could still feel Isaac's rough lips on mine.

Nate turned to me. "We'd better get going." He turned and strode down the driveway, kicking up gravel as he walked.

"Catch you later," Isaac said. "I've got to whip these guys into shape." He flashed me a strange smile. "Good luck on Fear Street, Lisa."

I gave him a quick wave, then turned to follow Nate. My mind was spinning. Isaac and Nate had been good friends for a long time. Isaac knew he shouldn't have kissed me.

It wasn't like a friendly kiss, either. It was too intense for that.

I knew Nate had seen us. What was he going to say about it?

Actually, Nate didn't say much as we made our way to

Fear Street. He kept his eyes straight ahead on the road, as if he didn't want to see me sitting beside him. It wasn't like him at all to be so silent, and he was making me more and more uncomfortable.

"Isaac was telling me about Fear Street," I said finally to break the silence. "Actually, he was warning me."

"I don't believe that stuff," Nate said, swerving to pass a school bus. "Everyone is so freaked out by the Fear family." He shook his head. "I'm not friends with Brendan Fear, but I think he's a good dude."

Brendan Fear was a senior at Shadyside High. I'd seen him in the halls, but I hadn't met him.

"Isaac said I shouldn't take the job because it's on Fear Street," I said.

Nate stared straight ahead. "Isaac reads too many comic books," he said.

That ended the conversation.

The sun went behind clouds as we turned onto Fear Street, and the sky darkened. Tall trees slanted over the street. The houses looked old. They had wide front yards and were set far back from the street.

A rabbit darted across the street in front of us, and Nate swung the wheel to miss it. "Whoa!" I cried out as I was swung against the passenger door. "My first dangerous moment on Fear Street," I joked.

But Nate didn't laugh. We passed a wooded lot. A tall, dark-shingled house came into view, set behind a low hedge. "What number is that?" I asked. "I think that's the house."

Nate hit the brake, and we crept past the driveway. The number on the mailbox was thirty-two. "Yes. That's it." I gazed up at it through the windshield. The house was completely dark except for an orangey light in the front window.

As we pulled up the drive, the front porch light flashed on. "Mrs. Hart must have been watching for me," I said. I straightened my hair. "Do I look okay?"

Nate finally turned to me. "Yeah. You look fine."

My chest suddenly felt fluttery. My hands were cold. "I can't believe I'm so nervous," I said. "Guess I really want the job."

"Piece of cake," Nate said. He leaned over and kissed my cheek. "Go get 'em."

My face tingled. I didn't expect him to kiss me. "I've got to pick up my brother at his piano lesson," he said. "I'll drop him back home. Then I'll swing back and get you."

I started to open the door. "Good luck," he called after me.

I took a deep breath and strode toward the brightly lit front porch.

15.

Brenda Hart pulled open the door before I rang the bell. "Lisa? Come in."

She pushed open the storm door and ushered me into the front hall. The house was warm and smelled of roast chicken. The walls were dark green. A tall brass lamp stood over a table with a stack of unopened mail on its top.

She shook hands with me. "Nice to meet you. I'm Brenda Hart." The front entryway opened into the living room. A steep wooden stairway led to the second floor. The living room had the same dark green walls. Two ceiling lights sent down a wash of pale light over the dark furniture, two armchairs behind a low coffee table, facing a steep-backed black leather couch. An open copy of *People* magazine lay on the couch.

Brenda motioned for me to take one of the chairs. She was a thin, pretty woman, probably in her late thirties. She had black hair pushed straight back and tied in a loose ponytail behind her head. Her eyes were dark, and the lines beneath them made her look tired.

She was dressed young. She had a short pleated skirt over black tights, and a long-sleeved cream-colored T-shirt. She sighed as she took the armchair next to me. "It's been a long day. I'm glad you came."

"Thank you," I said, clearing my throat. She seemed like a nice person. Why couldn't I get over my nervousness?

"Do you live nearby?" she asked.

I nodded. "My mom and I . . . we live on Village Road near the pond. We just moved to Shadyside. A few months ago."

Her dark eyes locked on mine. "Do you like it?"

"Yes," I said. "It's a little different from Shaker Heights. I mean, smaller. But I like the school. And I've made some friends."

She pulled a pack of sugarless gum from her T-shirt pocket and offered me a piece. I waved it away. She slid two pieces into her mouth. "I'm addicted to this stuff."

"I'm a Mentos freak," I confessed.

She let out a dry, almost silent laugh. Her dark eyes flashed.

"Let me tell you about the job," she said, leaning closer to me.

"It's babysitting, right?" I said. I suddenly realized I didn't see or hear a kid. The house was silent except for the soft tick of a large square clock on the mantelpiece. And I didn't see any toys or other evidence of a child in the house.

"It's a little more than babysitting," Brenda said. She settled back on the chair. "I'd better start at the beginning. I just got a new job, and the hours are kind of long."

"You mean you work late?" I asked.

She brushed back her ponytail. "Yes. Three days a week I don't get home till nine or ten. So . . . this is what I need, Lisa. I need someone to pick Harry up at four o'clock three days a week."

"How old is Harry?" I asked.

"Harry is eight going on thirty-five," she joked. She gave that dry, whispery laugh again. "Actually, he's a sweetheart. You'll love him." She drummed the arm of the chair. I noticed her long, perfect fingernails, a dark red.

"Harry has to be picked up at my sister's house," Brenda continued. She waved a hand. "It's a few blocks away. My sister Alice is homeschooling Harry, and she's just a terrific teacher."

"Nice," I said awkwardly. She was waiting for me to respond, and I didn't know what to say. I heard a creaking sound and turned toward the door.

Brenda sighed. "That's just the old stairway," she said. "It likes to creak and groan like an old man. You'll get used to it. I don't even hear it anymore. I had some carpenters out to look at it. But they said all old houses shift and groan."

I gazed at the stairway for a moment. The banister was smoothly polished dark wood. The steps had no carpet on them.

"So you pick up Harry at four," Brenda said. "You bring

him home. You help him with his homework. Sometimes Alice piles it on, even though he's only eight."

"Harry is a good student?" I asked.

"He likes to work," she answered. "He's very curious about all kinds of things." She chewed the gum for a while, studying me. "After homework, you give him dinner. Then entertain him for a while. He has an Xbox game he loves. He plays it for hours."

"That sounds like fun," I said.

"You put him to bed around eight. And wait till I get home at nine or ten." She leaned close again and put a hand on my wrist. "Is that too many hours for you, Lisa?"

"No," I said. "I don't think so. I can do my homework after Harry goes to bed."

She nodded. "If you can take the job, I'll pay you well. I'll be honest. I'm really desperate to find someone good. I'll pay you three hundred dollars a week."

Whoa! I thought maybe I hadn't heard correctly. "Three hundred a week?" I repeated.

She nodded.

This will really help our money problems, I thought. *We'll be fine till Mom can go back to work. Finally, I've had some good luck.*

"Does this sound like something you'd like to do?" she asked. She tugged at a loose strand of her dark hair.

"Definitely," I said. I wanted to jump up and down for joy. I couldn't wait to tell my mother the good news. "Definitely."

"Harry is quiet and very self-sufficient," Brenda said. "He'll let you do your homework. What year are you, Lisa?"

"Junior," I said.

"Have you started to look at colleges?"

I hesitated. "Well . . . my mom and I have had some bad luck. I think I'm going to have to work for at least a year before I can go away to school."

She nodded, her dark eyes locked on mine, studying me. "Well, I hope this job helps," she said. "You'll like Harry. He's a little moody at times, but he'll be very little trouble."

I gazed around the living room again. I still didn't see a single clue that an eight-year-old boy lived here.

"Can I meet Harry?" I said. "Is he home?"

"He's the kind of kid who needs his rest," she said. "I try to put him to bed early." She climbed to her feet. She adjusted the short skirt over her tights. "Come up to his room with me. I'll introduce you."

I followed her to the stairway. The old wooden steps creaked and groaned under our shoes as we climbed to the second floor.

Harry's room was at the end of a long, dimly lit hall. The carpet was thin and torn in places. I heard the soft *drip drip* of water from a small bathroom as we passed it.

Harry's door was closed. We stopped at the door and Brenda knocked softly.

No answer.

She pushed the door open slowly. To my surprise, the room was totally dark. No light of any kind.

"Harry, are you in here?" Brenda called softly. "Harry? Are you here?"

16.

Silence.

Then a lamp flickered on, and I could see the boy sitting up in his bed, blinking in surprise.

My first thought: He's adorable.

He was round-cheeked and blond, his hair tousled over his broad forehead. Squinting into the lamplight, I saw that he had big, blue eyes and a sweet angelic smile.

He didn't seem surprised to see a stranger in his room. Brenda led the way to the side of the bed. Despite the warm night, Harry wore flannel pajamas with *Star Wars* characters all over them.

"Harry, this is Lisa," Brenda said.

"Were you asleep? Why were you sitting in the dark?" I blurted out.

He brushed his hair off his forehead. "I like to make up movies in my mind," he said. He had a funny, scratchy voice.

"I like movies, too," I said, eager to ingratiate myself.

"Do you like *scary* movies?" he asked.

"Not really," I said. "I get too scared."

"Me too," he said, pointing a finger at his chest. "I don't like to be scared."

"Lisa is going to stay with you when I'm at work," Brenda said, straightening his striped quilt. "Would you like that?"

Harry's eyes grew wide. "Will you sing my favorite song to me?" he asked me.

I blinked. "Your favorite song? What is it?"

He grinned. "Eensy Weensy Spider."

"Huh? But that's a baby song!" I said.

His smile faded. "Not if it's about a *real spider*," he said in his scratchy voice.

Weird.

I turned to Brenda. "What is he talking about?"

"Harry likes to make jokes—don't you, Harry?"

"Not really," he said.

"So Lisa will pick you up at Alice's and take care of you when I'm at work," Brenda told him.

Harry turned his blue eyes on me. "Can we stay up late? *Can* we?"

Something about the desperate way he asked made me laugh.

"Well? Can we?" He really wanted an answer.

"I don't know," I said. "We'll see."

He tossed his fists in the air as if he'd won a victory. "Yes-sss!"

"Time to go to sleep," Brenda said, smoothing her hand

gently over his hair. "No more movies in your mind, okay? Just sleep."

"Okay." He settled his head on the pillow. "G'night, Lisa."

"Goodnight," I said. "See you soon, Harry."

We stepped back into the hall. Brenda closed the bedroom door behind us. "So you'll take the job?" she asked softly.

I nodded. "Yes. I can't imagine *anyone* saying no to Harry. He's a total angel."

I started to follow her to the stairway. But halfway down the hall, she turned and grabbed my wrist. "Listen," she said in a whisper. "Don't let Harry stay up late. Seriously. It's very bad for him. Don't *ever* let Harry stay up late."

17.

Nate kissed me lightly. I pressed my lips against his, harder. I wrapped my hands behind his head and held him there and kissed him until we couldn't breathe. I pulled my face back, my hands lingering in his hair.

"Finish the story," he said, nuzzling my cheek with his head.

We were wrapped around each other, on the couch facing the fireplace in my living room.

"So the mother told you not to let the kid stay up late," Nate said.

I nodded. "Yes. She said don't ever let him. And I said, why not? Does he have some kind of condition?"

"And what did she say?" Nate urged.

"She said no, he doesn't have a condition. He just needs more sleep than most kids. She said he gets very grouchy and he can't focus if he doesn't get eight hours sleep. Weird, right?"

"Wish I could get eight hours sleep," Nate said, sighing. "My brother is an early bird. He jumps on my bed to wake me up at six thirty in the morning for no reason."

"You should probably kill him," I said.

Nate laughed. He thinks I'm funny. He pulled me against him and we kissed some more. When the front doorbell rang, we both jumped up as if we'd been caught doing something wrong.

I brushed back my hair and hurried to open the door. Saralynn and Isaac walked in. "Don't talk to me. I'm in a really bad mood," Isaac said.

"Well, hello to you, too," I said. "Did you come over to put us *all* in a bad mood?"

"Definitely," he said. "Why should I be the only one?"

"He won't shut up about his band," Saralynn said. "I've begged him to stop talking about it. Begged and pleaded, but—"

"Somebody put me out of my misery," Isaac wailed. "No. Really. Shoot me now." He plopped down on the couch beside Nate.

"Isaac, what's up?" Nate said.

Isaac raised his fist and punched Nate really hard in the thigh. "Did that hurt?"

Nate uttered a cry and scooted to the other side of the couch. "Yeah, that hurt. Are you *crazy*?"

"That's the way my brain feels," Isaac said.

Nate rubbed his leg. "Since when did you get a brain?" he growled.

"My band has a gig Saturday night," Isaac said, ignoring Nate's insult. "You know. At the Hothouse. An actual paying job. And guess what? We're down to two members—me and the dopey kid from across the street who doesn't know which end of the drumsticks to hold."

"That's bad news," Nate said. "Remind me not to go see you Saturday night." Nate kept flashing Isaac angry looks. I wondered if he was thinking about Isaac kissing me in front of his garage.

I knew Nate had seen us. But he still hadn't said a word about it to me.

Isaac growled again and turned away from the three of us. He buried his head in his hands and muttered curses to himself. He likes to be as overdramatic as he can.

"Can we talk about something else?" Saralynn said. "How was your first day back at school, Lisa?"

"Not bad," I said. "Everyone was really nice. I was so happy to be back. I didn't even mind Mr. Trevalian's horrible jokes."

"He thinks he's a riot," Saralynn said. "He probably gets his jokes from kindergarten books. What did the apple say to the ground? I think I'm falling for you."

"That doesn't even make sense," Isaac muttered.

"I hope Lisa didn't go back to school too soon." We all turned as my mom came walking into the room. She carried a tall blue vase of yellow tulips to the coffee table in her good arm. "I don't want her to put extra pressure on herself. She needs to recover in good time."

"It was Dr. Shein's idea, Mom," I snapped. "I'm back at school, so stop fretting about it."

I found myself getting easily annoyed at my mother the past few days. She never used to be a worrier. She was always the calm, unemotional one in the family. But since the accident, she fretted about every little thing, and she was always totally negative and disturbing about anything that happened.

I wanted to get better and go on with my life. I didn't want to mope around and worry that I shouldn't try things.

Mom set the tulips down and fussed over them for a few seconds. "Did Lisa tell you about her job? It's such good news for us. Especially since I can't go back to the salon because of this." She waved her cast in the air.

"Lisa will be an awesome nanny," Saralynn said. "That kid is lucky. He—"

"But the job is on Fear Street," Mom interrupted, shaking her head. "I'm just not sure about that."

"Stop it, Mom," I said. "Stop trying to discourage me. It was Dr. Shein's idea, remember? She thinks I can handle it. Let me give it a try. Besides, since when are you so superstitious?"

Mom flinched. I could see that my question hurt her. But I didn't care. I was starting a new part of my life, and I needed encouragement, not more doubt.

Everyone went home a short while later. Isaac said he was going to beg his friends to come back to the band. Nate kissed me quickly and said he'd be glad to drive me to my new job the next day after school. Saralynn said to call later if I needed her.

I went to my room to do some reading for English class. But before I could find the assignment, the phone rang. I didn't recognize the number on the phone, but I answered it anyway. "Hello?"

"Lisa? It's Summer Lawson."

Summer Lawson? It took me a few seconds to remember her. A tall, copper-haired girl in my Government class, very pretty, with high cheekbones like a fashion model, always wears a lot of clanky plastic bracelets and beads and long dangling earrings. Has a lot of attitude and style.

Summer Lawson. My mind whirred, trying to remember more. She was Nate's girlfriend. Yes. Before me. What broke them up? I didn't really know.

"Hey, Summer," I said. "What's up?"

There was a long silence. Then she replied. "Do you know you're in major trouble?" Her voice was cold. Flat.

"Excuse me?" I said. "What kind of trouble?"

"Lisa," she said, "do you have any clue about Nate?"

"Huh? I-I really don't know what you're talking about," I stammered.

"You'll find out," she said.

A loud click ended the conversation.

18.

After school the next day, I felt kind of shaky, tense about my new job. As I walked up the driveway to Brenda's sister's house, I saw Harry in the front window. The sunlight caught his blond hair and made him glow like an angel.

This is going to be fun, I told myself.

Alice's house was small and square, painted white with dark green shutters at the windows. A racing bike leaned against the side wall. Spring flowers in large pots on both sides of the front stoop hadn't yet opened their buds.

Across the street, a boy kept throwing a tennis ball onto the slanted roof of his house, then catching it as it rolled off. I saw a red kite caught in the high limbs of a tree at the neighbors' driveway.

I stepped onto the front stoop and the front door swung open. Alice greeted me with a smile and waved me inside. She looked like an older version of Brenda. Her cheeks and forehead were lined. Her hair was cut short, streaks of gray with the black. She wore maroon sweats and carried a *Harry Potter* book in one hand.

"Lisa, it's so nice to meet you." We shook hands. Her hand was warm and soft. "Brenda told me all about you. I understand you've already met Harry."

Harry ran up to me and tugged at my arm. "Can we stay up late tonight? Can we?"

I laughed. Alice frowned and shook her head. "How about saying hello first, Harry?"

"Hello," Harry said. "Can we stay up late?"

"No, you cannot," Alice said firmly. "Don't try to take advantage of Lisa because she's new. Remember, Lisa is the boss. Can you remember that?"

"Maybe," Harry replied.

Alice waved the book in front of her. "I've started to read him his first *Harry Potter* book. You're enjoying it, aren't you, Harry?"

He nodded. "I like him because his name is Harry."

"That's a good name," I said. "Would you like me to borrow the book from Alice and read you a few chapters tonight?"

"No," he replied quickly. "I want to watch cartoons."

Alice rubbed a hand through his hair. "Don't forget you have homework to do first."

"I already forgot," Harry said. He laughed. He was making a joke. His blue eyes twinkled.

"Go get your backpack," Alice told him. "It's in my bedroom."

When Harry left the room, she pulled me aside and spoke in a confidential tone. "He stayed up late last night. That's very bad for him. He's a beast when he doesn't get his sleep. Be sure to get him to bed early."

"No problem," I said. "He seems very sweet."

"He is," Alice said, her eyes on the hallway, watching for Harry to return. "He's a good student, too. He learns quickly, and he really likes to learn new things."

"That's awesome," I whispered back.

Alice placed a hand on my shoulder. "Eight-year-olds can be a challenge, though, even if they're as sweet as Harry. If you have any problems at all, just call me." She reached into the pocket of her sweatpants and handed me a slip of paper with her phone number on it.

"Thanks," I said.

"I don't think you'll have problems with him. But just in case . . ."

I started to thank her again. But I stopped when I heard a shrill cry. A tiny voice. Was it coming from the basement?

Startled, I listened hard. It sounded like a sob.

"Mister Puffball—be quiet!" Alice shouted. She laughed and shook her head. "My cat is very good at letting me know when he's hungry."

"Oh, wow," I said. "It didn't sound like a cat."

Alice laughed again. "Mister Puffball *can communicate really well*—especially at dinnertime."

I smiled. But the cry I heard didn't sound at all like a cat. It sounded human.

19.

"Can I sit on your lap?"

Harry had to be the sweetest, friendliest eight-year-old in the world. By the time he finished his mac and cheese dinner, he and I were already BFF's. He was funny and smart. He whipped through his homework, about six pages of math problems.

His big joke of the night: He'd tug at my hair and make a different sound effect each time. For some reason, he thought that was a riot. But when I tugged his hair and made an *oink oink* sound, he said it wasn't funny at all.

He kept begging me to stay up late. "Maybe some other night. Not tonight," I answered. That seemed to satisfy him—until ten minutes later, when he'd ask me again.

He sat on my lap, and we watched *Kung Fu Panda 2* on Netflix. The cartoon made him laugh. A couple of times he leapt to the floor and did some crazy kung fu moves.

When the movie ended, I glanced at the time. Nearly eight o'clock. "Bedtime," I told him.

"I have a panda upstairs," he said. "In my closet. Maybe I could bring him down. We could do our own panda movie."

"Not tonight," I insisted.

"A short one?"

"No. Not tonight. I see what you're doing, Harry. You're stalling. Come on. Let's get you in your pajamas."

After that, he was no problem. We got him changed and tucked in. I said goodnight. He asked me to close his door, so I did.

Downstairs, I washed the dinner dishes. Then I sat down on the living room couch to read my English assignment, a short story by an author I'd never heard of, Willa Cather. I'm not too interested in farm life, so the story was pretty boring.

I was glad when my phone rang and it was Nate. "What's up? How's the kid?" he asked.

"He's awesome," I said. "Maybe the most adorable kid in the world."

"Sweet. What did you give him for dinner? Frosted Flakes?"

I laughed. "No way. I made him mac and cheese. Right out of the box. It's his favorite. The kid is so easy, this job is a breeze."

"Nice," Nate said. "I'm just checking in. You know, see how it's going."

"Hey, I have to ask you something," I said. "I had this weird phone call from Summer Lawson."

"Huh? Summer? You're kidding."

"It was totally awkward and strange, Nate. I think she was calling to warn me about you."

"About me?" He snickered. "Yeah, I'm real dangerous. I'm a real dangerous dude."

"Well, why did she call me?" I demanded.

"How should I know?" he snapped. "She's crazy."

"No. Really—"

"She's crazy, Lisa," he said. "Ask anyone. And she's a total troublemaker."

I heard a crackling in my ear. "Hey, where are you?" I asked. "It doesn't sound like you're home."

He hesitated. "I'm . . . uh . . . out."

"Where? Are you nearby?"

"Kind of," he said.

Why is he being so weird? Why won't he tell me where he is?

"Did you hear about Isaac?" he said. "He convinced his friends to come back to the band."

"Amazing," I said. "How did he convince them?"

"He said he'd divide up the money they make at the club Saturday night evenly."

"That's all it took?"

"I guess," Nate said. "They'll still suck but at least Isaac won't be standing up there with that twelve-year-old drummer."

"It's a shame about the band," I said. "Isaac is a good guitar player." *Isaac kissed me. Isaac kissed me and Nate saw.* That moment played again in my mind.

"Maybe we should go see him Saturday night," I said.

"Maybe," Nate replied. *Was he thinking about that kiss, too?*

We talked a little longer. Then I returned to the short story. Not much happened in the story. It seemed to be mostly description of the wheat fields and the dry, flat plains around the farm.

After a while, my eyelids began to feel heavy. I think maybe I drifted off to sleep for a little while.

Then a noise jolted me awake. The book fell from my lap and bounced on the carpet. I heard the noise again. A tapping. From upstairs?

"Harry?" I called. "Is that you?"

I jumped to my feet and turned to the stairway. "Harry? Are you still awake? It's late."

No reply.

Silence.

I jumped as the floor up there creaked from footsteps. "Harry? Are you walking around up there? Answer me. Harry?"

My heart started to pound as I made my way to the stairway.

I gazed into the dim light at the top—and gasped in horror.

20.

I saw a blur of light. Two legs. A shadowy figure. Darting across the landing.

Was it a man? An intruder?

"Hey—stop!" I choked out a cry. My heart was thudding so hard, I thought my chest might explode. "Stop! I see you!"

I should have called 911. But I didn't think. I saw the intruder flash across the landing heading toward Harry's room. I grabbed the banister and pulled myself up the steep stairs.

"Stop! Who are you? What are you *doing* here?" I screamed all the way up.

My legs trembling, my chest aching, I reached the landing. I gazed down the long hall. Harry's door was wide open.

"No! Stop! Get out of there!" I screamed in a hoarse voice I'd never heard before.

My shoes caught on the ragged carpet as I lowered my

head and ran down the hall. I stumbled and nearly fell to my knees. Regained my balance and kept running.

"Harry?" I shouted. "Are you okay?"

No answer.

I burst into his room, gasping for breath. The room was dark. The only light came from the open window. And in that gray light, I saw the intruder. His back to me as he thundered to the window. Lowered his head.

And leaped out.

Leaped out a second-story window.

He didn't make a sound.

I bolted to the window and stuck my head out. The air felt cool against my burning-hot face. I peered down into the yard, squinting in the pale light. And I saw a twisted shadow scrabbling across the grass.

The man bent over, legs bent like insect legs, moving to the deep shadow at the back of the yard.

I gripped the windowsill tightly and watched as he ran. And just before he reached the black blanket of shadow, he turned. He turned and his face caught the moonlight.

And I screamed again. Because his face wasn't human. It was the ugly, twisted face of a demon-creature from a horror movie. Green skin. A lightbulb-shaped bald scalp with a thick stripe of black fur down the middle and sharp pig ears poking up from the sides. Blood-red eyes glaring like headlights over a long wolfish snout.

"Nooooooooo." A low moan escaped my throat. I knew I was hallucinating again.

The same creature I saw when I was sleepwalking in the woods. I was seeing it again. I was seeing something that wasn't there. Hallucinating a demon again. Insane. Insane.

"No. Oh, please. No."

I turned to the bed. "Harry? Are you okay? Harry?"

He wasn't there.

21.

I froze, staring at the empty bed, the covers tossed to the floor. I clicked on the ceiling light. I stood there unable to move. Unable to think straight.

Total panic.

And a million thoughts raced through my mind at once.

The intruder was real, not an hallucination. He was wearing a mask. Like the monster mask Nate wore for Saralynn's video. Like the dozens of monster masks in Nate's collection.

He was real. He wore a mask. He was in this room. I didn't make him up. I saw him.

Did he grab Harry? Pull Harry from his bed and leap out the window with him?

How was that possible?

Get a grip, Lisa. Get control. Get control.

I struggled to slow down my furious breathing. I turned away from the empty bed.

Think. Got to think clearly.

"Harry? Harry?" I shouted his name. Maybe he was still in the house. Maybe he could hear me.

"Harry? Are you here?" *Please—be here.*

But no reply.

I stumbled out into the hall and gazed up and down. "Harry? Are you here? Please answer me! Harry?"

No. No. The panic had me in its grip. I knew I had to try to clear my head and act rationally. But the hallway was tilting and spinning. I could barely breathe.

"Harry! Harry! Harry!"

I knew what I had to do. I had to call the police.

My phone. Where was my phone?

Downstairs. On the living room couch. I hurled myself down the stairs. I ran into the living room. Grabbed my bag off the couch. Frantically pawed through it for the phone.

Where is it? Where?

I heard a knocking sound. Very nearby. The bag fell from my hand. I heard scraping. Another knock. A soft thud.

Someone is in the house.

I could feel the panic tighten its grip on me. I couldn't think. I couldn't breathe.

Someone was at the front of the house.

The masked intruder had returned.

22.

*A*nother soft *thud*.

I stood frozen by the couch, my bag at my feet, and listened.

It sounded like knocking. Someone knocking on the front door?

Without thinking, I lurched to the entryway. No one there. No one in the house.

The knocking sounds again.

I turned. The coat closet! The sounds were coming from the coat closet! "Who's there?" I tried to shout but the words came out in a choked whisper. "Who—?"

I stepped to the closet, yanked open the door—and gasped. "Harry? What are *you* doing in here?" I cried.

He stood huddled against the back wall, surrounded by coats. His whole body was trembling, and his face was as pale as flour. "I'm scared," he said in a tiny voice.

I reached for him with both hands, and he let me pull him from the closet. The poor little kid was shaking so hard.

I lifted him up and held him close until the shivers seemed to end.

"S-someone came into my room," he stammered. "Someone scared me. So I ran . . . to the closet."

"It's okay," I said, smoothing back his blond hair. His pale forehead was drenched with sweat. "It's okay now."

I led him to the couch. He wanted to sit on my lap. I tugged him up and wrapped my arms around him. "Did you see the man?" I asked. "Did you see his face?"

Harry shook his head. "It was too dark. I didn't really see him. I . . . heard someone . . . in my room. So I ran. Downstairs. And I hid in the closet."

I suddenly had an idea, a way to calm Harry. "Maybe it was a nightmare," I said. "Maybe it was just a bad dream you were having."

I was lying, of course. But if it would calm him down and make him feel safe . . .

He looked up at me with those big blue eyes. "Really? You think I was dreaming?"

I nodded. "Yes. We all have nightmares. I have nightmares a lot. But then I wake up and everything is fine."

He stared at me, thinking about it. "Maybe," he said finally. "It *felt* kind of like a nightmare."

He nestled his head against my shoulder, and we sat there in silence for a while. I pictured the intruder again, with the ugly strip of fur down his misshapen head. Once again I pictured him leaping from Harry's bedroom window and scrambling across the backyard. I saw his face in the moonlight as he turned and stared up at me. The wolfish snout. The twisted, hideous face.

Was it a mask? Like that horror-movie mask Nate wore? No. No way.

Why would someone put on a mask, break into the house, run upstairs, and leap out a window?

It was totally crazy. It made no sense at all.

I was glad I lied to Harry. I was glad that maybe I convinced him the whole thing was a bad dream.

It felt like a bad dream to me, too. But I knew better.

After a few minutes, I realized that Harry had fallen asleep on my lap. He was snoring gently, his head still pressed against me. My legs started to ache. He began to feel heavy. But I didn't want to move him.

I sat there holding onto him, and maybe I dozed off, too. Because the next thing I knew, I felt a gentle tap on my shoulder. I blinked. Turned my head. And saw Brenda gazing down on me.

"Oh. Hi," I managed, trying to wake up.

She had dark rings around her eyes. Her lipstick had faded. Her hair was tousled. She smiled at me. "I guess you and Harry have bonded already," she said.

"He . . . had a nightmare," I said. "He came downstairs so I could comfort him."

"That's wonderful, Lisa." She set down her briefcase. "Harry is usually shy with new people."

"No. We had a good time," I said. "I think we're going to be pals."

Brenda helped lift him off my lap. Harry woke up groggily and eyed his mother without speaking. I climbed off the couch and helped Brenda get him to his feet. Then we half-carried him, half-walked him up the stairs to his room.

After we deposited him in his bed, we returned to the living room. I picked my bag up off the floor.

Brenda yawned. She brushed her hair back. "I'm exhausted," she said, sighing. "Long hours." She turned to me. "So, everything went fine?"

My mind spun.

No. It didn't go fine. There was an intruder in the house with the face of a demon. He ran into Harry's room and leaped out of the second-story window.

Everything wasn't fine. In fact, it was terrifying—for me and for Harry.

But if I tell Brenda the truth . . . If I tell her about the demon-creature in the house . . . she probably won't believe me. She'll think I'm crazy, and I'll lose this job.

I need this job. I really need it.

"Yes," I said. "No problems. Everything went fine. Harry is a total sweetheart."

23.

My mother waited up for me. I found her in the den in her gray flannel nightshirt, with the TV blasting, an old Denzel Washington movie on the screen. Mom is a Denzel Washington freak. I mean, she watches the same movies with him over and over. She doesn't care what movie it is.

"Mom, why is that so loud?" I said, covering my ears.

"To keep me awake," she said. "I wanted to stay up to hear about your first day on the job."

Oh, wow.

She raised the remote and muted the sound. She had a tall glass of light beer on the table next to her chair. Mom doesn't like wine. She only drinks light beer. She took a long sip of the beer, then adjusted the sling over her other arm.

"So? Spill," she ordered. "How did it go?"

I couldn't hold back. I knew I shouldn't tell her the truth. After all, I hadn't told Brenda Hart the truth. But I dropped down on the couch facing her, and it all just tumbled out of me in a long stream of words. I don't think I took a breath.

As I talked, her face became more and more drawn. She raised the glass but didn't take a drink, just held it in mid-air as she listened to my horror story.

When I finished, I sank back against the couch, breathing hard, watching her, waiting for her reaction.

Mom set the glass down and leaned forward, her good hand gripping the chair arm. She squinted at me, studying me. "He had a monster face?" she said finally. "Like a demon? You mean he was wearing a Halloween mask?"

"I-I don't know," I stammered. "It *had* to be a mask—right? I mean, I know Fear Street is supposed to be this scary place. But give me a break. There aren't *demons* running around in the houses there."

Mom let out a sigh. "And you say he jumped out a window? You saw him jump out a window?"

I suddenly realized why she was questioning me like that. "You don't believe me—do you?" I jumped to my feet. "You think it was another hallucination. You think I was seeing things again, right? Right?"

"Sit down, Lisa." She motioned me down with her one good hand. "Please. Sit down. I *thought* it might be too soon for you to take a job."

"Mom, don't start—" I said.

"Too soon," she repeated, shaking her head. "I'm so sorry, Lisa."

"Mom, please. I know what I saw."

"Lisa, listen to me," she said, avoiding my eyes. "If you're still seeing things, I . . . I think you should quit."

"I'm *not* seeing things!" I shrieked. I leaped to my feet again. My arms swung out. I gasped as I hit the table lamp hard and sent it toppling off the table.

It crashed to the floor and shattered, sending shards of glass flying.

"Oh, noo," I moaned.

Mom's face was twisted in horror. "You're out of control!" she screamed. "Do you see what I mean? Look what you've done. You're not responsible, Lisa. You're not responsible. You need more help!"

My chest was heaving up and down. "It was an accident. A stupid accident!" I cried. "Forget about the lamp. I know what I saw at that house, Mom. Stop trying to make me feel like I'm insane or something."

"I didn't say that, Lisa. Take a breath. Try to calm down. It seems clear that you're still seeing things."

"Mom, Harry saw him, too!" I screamed. "I'm not crazy. I didn't imagine the intruder. Harry saw him, too."

She blinked. I could see she was thinking hard. "The boy saw him, too? He saw a man with a demon face?"

"Well . . . no," I said. "I mean, Harry said he *heard* someone. He didn't see him. It was too dark. But he heard him. He heard him come into his room."

Mom stared at me. She didn't say anything. But I could read her thoughts. I could see on her face that she didn't believe me.

"I'm not crazy, Mom!" I screamed. "You've got to believe me."

"But, Lisa, stop and think," she said softly. She hates it when I scream. "It doesn't make sense. It was late. You were tired. And so you saw something that—"

"Shut up!" I cried. "Shut up! Just shut up! If *you* don't believe me, *someone* will! Just shut up and leave me alone!"

I stormed out of the den, swinging my fists, stomping over the glass shards of the broken lamp. I was gritting my teeth so hard, my jaw ached. I felt angry and frustrated— and alone.

As I reached the stairs to go up to my room, Mom poked her head out of the den. Even from a distance, I could see she had tears in her eyes, tear tracks running down her cheeks.

"Lisa, you're not the only one who's going through a bad time," she said, her voice cracking. "We're all alone now, just the two of us. Your father is gone. We need to stick together."

I knew I should apologize. I knew I should try to lose my anger. I knew the right thing to do, but I just couldn't do it.

"How can we stick together if you don't believe anything I say?" I shouted. I didn't wait for an answer. I didn't want to hear her answer. I turned and bolted up the stairs two at a time.

I slammed the door to my room. Then I jumped onto the bed and pulled my phone from my bag.

I need someone to believe me.

I need someone who doesn't think I'm a nutcase.

I punched Nate's number on the phone. He answered after the second ring. "Lisa? What's up?"

I told the whole story again. When I reached the part about the intruder with the demon face, I heard him sigh. "Lisa, you sound terrible. Take a breath. You really need to chill."

"You don't believe me, either, do you, Nate?"

Silence. Then he said, "Why don't I come over? Would that be good? Would you like some company? I could come over."

"You don't believe me—do you?" I insisted. "Nate, you think I'm crazy, too. Don't you, Nate? *Don't* you!"

24.

D r. Shein usually sat behind her glass desk, tapping
her pencil on the desktop or chewing on the eraser
while I talked. But today she paced back and forth along
the curtained window that stretched over one side of her
office.

She wore a summery, long pleated skirt, pale blue, and
a long-sleeved white blouse, the soft collar loose at her
throat. A gold locket swung on a slender chain as she walked.

She nodded her head but had no expression that I could
read as I told her about my first night at Harry's house. But
she stopped walking and crossed her arms in front of her
when I came to the part about the demon-creature leaping out the window.

I finished telling her about Harry hiding in the closet
and about how I decided not to tell Brenda what had happened. Dr. Shein slid back into her desk chair and pulled
herself close to the desk. She scribbled some notes on a
yellow pad, her head bent over her work.

I waited to hear her reaction.

Was she going to be like Mom and Nate and not believe I saw what I saw?

Finally, she raised her head and set down her pencil. "This is all going to take time, Lisa," she said softly.

I stared at her. Did this mean she didn't believe me?

"Your brain suffered a terrible shock," she continued. "This has resulted in vivid nightmares, as we both know. And sometimes, your nightmares have been so vivid, they have seemed to come to life."

"Does this mean—" I started.

But she cut me off with a quick wave of her hand. "You saw something at the Hart house that triggered a frightening image in your subconscious," she said. "These episodes are not hard to understand and are not unusual."

"Episodes?" I said.

She nodded, still toying with the locket.

"You don't think I saw what I saw?" I demanded, my voice growing shrill.

"I think you saw *something*," she replied. "I know you're not making it up, and I know you're not crazy. It's our job to get you past these episodes, to make you feel stronger and less afraid. That's why I'm going to suggest a couple of medications I think will help you, dear."

My chest suddenly felt all fluttery. "Medication? But isn't that a step backward?"

"No, not at all," she replied, shaking her head. "We have all kinds of things we can try to get you back on track."

She tapped the pencil eraser on the glass desktop. "You have to understand what's happening, Lisa. The accident jarred all kinds of feelings loose from your subconscious. Feelings of guilt because of losing your father. Feelings of extreme fear. That's where this creature you saw is coming from."

I opened my mouth to disagree, but changed my mind.

"This isn't unusual," she continued. "I don't want you to be afraid. If you feel you would like to try it, I can prescribe some drugs that calm you a bit. They might make it easier to get through a day without these disturbing fantasies."

"I don't know. I—"

"I'd never prescribe anything unless you were comfortable with it," she said. "Go home and think about it. Discuss it with your mother. I want you to be completely fine with anything we do to get you over this."

She bent her head again and concentrated on writing notes on the yellow pad. This meant our session was over.

I stood up but I didn't leave. I felt as if my brain was ready to explode. I wanted to keep talking to her. I wanted to ask a hundred questions. I wanted to tell her that I knew I *wasn't* hallucinating at Harry's house. What I saw was real.

I saw the creature's face too clearly for it to be imaginary. I saw it leap out the bedroom window. I heard the *thud* as it landed in the backyard.

I needed Dr. Shein to believe me. Mom didn't believe me. Nate didn't believe me. She was my last hope.

"See you in two days," I muttered and made my way out the door.

I don't think I ever felt so alone. Would I be able to persuade Dr. Shein in our next session? Could I convince her I was getting better? My mind was getting clearer? I knew the difference between hallucinations and what was real.

At least, I thought I did.

Until I returned home—and had another insane hallucination.

I stepped into the living room. Blinding yellow sunlight flooded the room from the front windows. I raised one hand to shield my eyes from the glare—and imagined—for the hundredth time—that Morty was sprawled on the living room carpet.

I uttered a sharp cry. *Isn't this ever going to stop?*

But the shocks weren't over.

25.

I tried to blink the image of the big, white dog away, but I couldn't get it to disappear. The dog rolled onto its haunches. Its eyes caught the sunlight and flared bright red.

And then my hallucination came running toward me, big paws padding the carpet, furry tail swinging hard behind it. I didn't realize the dog was real until he leaped onto me, forcing me to stumble back onto the couch. And then he was licking my face, and I screamed.

"Morty? Morty? Is it really you?"

Mom came into the room, carrying a large pot of geraniums. "I was next door," she said. "I didn't get a chance to tell you the good news."

"It's really Morty?" I cried. I gently shoved him away before he licked all the skin off my cheeks. "Is it?"

"A nice young woman found him on the highway near Martinsville," Mom said. "She brought him back while you were at the doctor's."

"I can't *believe* it!" I screamed. I hugged Morty around

the neck and held him close to me. "See, Mom? Things are definitely turning around for me."

"I hope," she murmured softly.

"You must be feeling better," Saralynn said. "I didn't think you'd come with us tonight."

"She's a glutton for punishment," Nate said, behind the wheel. He turned the car onto the River Road. The three of us were on our way to hear Isaac's band.

The sun had gone down, leaving a blue evening tint over everything. Tall trees leaned over the curving road, blocking the moonlight, making it appear that we were driving over deep puddles of darkness.

"I just felt like getting out of the house and hearing some music," I said.

"Music? Then why come see Isaac's band?" Nate joked. He put an arm around my shoulder and tugged me toward him.

"Drive with two hands, please," I said.

"They've been rehearsing like crazy," Saralynn said from the backseat. "Maybe they got better."

"Maybe I won't need the earplugs I brought," Nate said.

"You have a bad attitude," I said.

Once again, I pictured Isaac kissing me in his driveway. Was Nate watching? Was that why Nate was so down on Isaac lately? His jokes about Isaac were all nasty and hostile, as if they hadn't been best friends for years.

"I offered to give the whole band Frankenstein masks

from my collection," Nate said. "They could call themselves The Young Frankensteins or something. See? That way, when they played, no one could see their faces. So they wouldn't have to be embarrassed by how bad they were."

"Nice guy," Saralynn said sarcastically.

"Stop making jokes," I told Nate. "We're going there to support Isaac."

He grunted something I didn't hear. We drove on for a while, following the road as it curved along the Conononká River. The dark water flowed silently beside us, occasionally glimmering under silvery moonlight.

"The club won't sell beer to anyone under eighteen," Nate said. "But I brought a fake ID that's worked before. Try to look old."

"That's why I put my hair up," Saralynn said. She had dressed in her club outfit—a short, red pleated skirt over silver tights, a shiny vest over a silky silver top.

I don't have a club outfit. I wore a silky gold-colored top over jeans that had rhinestones on the pockets. "I look twelve. I can't help it," I said, sighing.

"Well, try not to be conspicuous," Nate said. "They won't care tonight. It's going to be all kids from our school."

He turned into the wide, paved driveway. The Hothouse is one of three clubs close together on the River Road. It's a music club—not a dance club. They usually book two or three bands a night. On most nights, you have to be eighteen to get in. But on nights when they have a teen band, they open the place up to high school students.

It was early. We knew Isaac's band was going on first. I saw only four or five cars in the parking lot. For Isaac's sake, I hoped more kids would come.

We climbed out of the car. Hip-hop music rang out from speakers on high poles around the lot. The neon Hothouse sign crackled as we stepped around it to get to the front entrance.

We each paid a five-dollar cover charge to a guy at the front door with a shaved head and an awesome tattoo sleeve of snakes and dragons. Inside, the lights pulsed, red then black, red then black. The walls and ceiling were red. The banquettes along the sides were red. You get the idea. The place had a very basic color scheme.

The aroma of beer floated over the club. Three or four people waited in line for drinks at the bar at the back. Peering into the blinking foggy light, I recognized some kids from school at one of the banquettes and waved.

The stage was a square, open area at the far end of the club. Isaac and his friends were setting up, hooking their instruments to the club amps and speakers.

When Isaac saw us walk in, he came trotting over. He wore faded jeans ripped to shreds at the knees and a black-and-red Daft Punk T-shirt. He bumped knuckles with Nate, then turned to Saralynn and me.

"Hey, Lisa, I didn't think you'd come," he said.

"I didn't want to miss it," I said. "This is totally exciting, Isaac."

"Who are those guys over there?" Nate asked, pointing to four or five guys entering from a back door, carrying instruments.

Isaac turned and squinted into the pulsing red light. "They must be the dudes in Psycho-Relic. It's a seventies tribute band."

"They any good?" Nate asked.

Isaac shrugged. "Never listened to them. But the club told us we could only do two songs tonight so their band can go on early."

Nate snickered. "Do you *know* two songs?"

"Not really," Isaac said, grinning. "We have one song that we don't totally suck at, and then we play different versions of it."

It wasn't hot in the club, but Isaac had sweat glistening his forehead. His eyes kept returning to me, as if he was trying to tell me something. Or maybe he was just genuinely surprised to see me.

Saralynn gazed around. "Hope more kids come."

"They'll start coming in for Psycho-Relic," Isaac said. "A lot of kids are into that retro stuff. And the band has some YouTube videos that get a lot of hits."

Back at the stage area, I heard a loud *pop*. One of the amps erupted in a burst of yellow current, and the guy working on it jumped back with a startled cry.

"I'd better get back there and help before my guys electrocute themselves," Isaac said.

"That would be an awesome opening," Nate said.

Isaac ignored him. He gave us a quick wave and took off. "Later."

I saw more kids from school drifting into the club. Kerry Reacher was walking toward the stage with Eric Finn. I looked for Patti Berger but I didn't see her. Patti and Kerry are like Siamese twins. They're never apart.

A group of four or five girls walked in together. They weren't from Shadyside High. One of them had dyed pink hair and wore a purple-and-yellow Psycho-Relics sweatshirt.

Nate came up behind me and slid his arms around my waist. He nuzzled the back of my neck. It sent a chill down my back.

I leaned back against him. I felt a wave of happiness wash over me. It felt good to be out of the house and out with friends.

Saralynn tugged Nate away. "Are you going to get us beers or not?" she demanded.

Nate glanced around. "It isn't crowded enough. We'll be caught," he said. He started to the bar. "Will you settle for a Coke?"

Saralynn rolled her eyes. "Living large."

I laughed, watching him stride toward the bar. "I never knew Nate was such a chicken."

Saralynn didn't smile. "He got caught once," she said. "Last year. With a fake ID. He got in a lot of trouble. His parents had to pull some strings to keep him from a juvenile hearing downtown."

I blinked at her. "Seriously? I didn't know that."

"There's a lot about Nate you don't know," she said.

I stared at her. *What a weird thing to say.* Why was she trying to prove that she knew more about Nate than I did?

There was definitely something I didn't know about going on here. Of course, I was new in town. Saralynn and I had been friends for only a month. We spent hours talking, but I suddenly realized I didn't know much about her.

Was she more interested in Nate than she let on?

Nate returned with the Cokes. On the stage, Isaac and his band picked up their instruments. "Hey, everyone," Isaac shouted into the mike, "we're The Black Holes and we came to rock your world!"

They began to play. The music was amped so loud, the floor vibrated, and I could feel the beats in my chest. Isaac's lead guitar soared and wailed and roared. He lifted his face to the ceiling and played, his eyes shut tight.

Nate had one hand around my waist. With his other hand, he flashed a thumbs-down. Then he stuck his finger down his throat and made a gagging sound.

He was right. The band was terrible. Even the deafening sound level vibrating in your ears couldn't hide the fact that the guys didn't seem to be playing the same song.

At least twenty or thirty people stood and watched and listened. When the number ended, we all cheered and clapped and pretended we were into it. Isaac didn't wait. He went into the next song. It sounded a lot like the first.

"This is painful!" Nate shouted in my ear.

This number went on for at least fifteen minutes. I had a feeling the band didn't know how to end it. What made Isaac think they were ready to perform in public?

When the music stopped, my ears were ringing. The club had become crowded. A lot of people had come to hear the Psycho-Relics.

I pushed toward the stage. Isaac and his friends were unhooking their instruments. Isaac didn't look happy.

I couldn't get through the crush of people. I bumped a girl and almost made her spill her beer. I waved to Isaac but he had his head down and didn't see me.

I turned and realized I'd gotten separated from Nate and Saralynn. Peering into the pulsing red lights, I couldn't find them.

A hand grabbed my wrist. "Nate?"

No.

I turned and saw Summer Lawson gazing at me. Her coppery hair fell loose to her shoulders. Her green eyes reflected the flashing club lights.

She wore a white shirt with most of the buttons open, over a short straight black skirt and black tights. As usual, she had on an assortment of colorful plastic necklaces and long, dangling plastic earrings.

Every time I see her, my first thought is how beautiful she is. Like some kind of goddess. Seriously.

"Summer?" I tried to tug my hand away, but she held onto it.

She brought her face close to my ear. Her perfume smelled

citrusy, like grapefruit or maybe lemon. "We need to talk, Lisa."

Again, I tried to free my hand. Finally, she let go. "What do you mean?" I shouted over the loud voices. "What's wrong, Summer?"

"We need to talk," she repeated. "Seriously. About Nate."

"Nate? What about Nate?" I cried.

Her eyes appeared to darken. She pressed her lips close to my ear. "You're in trouble, Lisa, and you don't know it."

Someone bumped me from behind, and I stumbled into Summer. "Sorry," I murmured.

I spun around to see Nate making his way around a couple of guys in gray hoodies. When I turned back, Summer had vanished.

Weird.

Nate stepped up beside me and handed me a fresh Coke. "Was that Summer?"

I nodded.

He narrowed his eyes at me. "What did she want?"

I shrugged. "Beats me. I don't know what her problem is. But she really creeps me out. She keeps warning me about you."

Nate laughed. "Maybe she just wants to tell you how awesome I am." He slid his arm around my waist and started to lead me to the exit. "Don't even think about her, Lisa," he said. "She's just jealous. That's all."

He brought his face close and kissed me, a long, sweet kiss.

It wasn't jealousy, I thought. *It really was a warning. She's trying to tell me I'm in trouble.*

Suddenly, Nate's lips felt cold to me. And I couldn't keep a frightened shiver from rolling down my back.

26.

Monday afternoon, a gray cool day threatening rain, I picked up Harry at his aunt Alice's house. I found them in the kitchen. Harry was on his knees on a tall stool, a spatula in hand, stirring the dark contents of a big bowl.

"We're making brownies," Alice said. "Well, actually, Harry is making brownies. I'm just helping."

Harry dipped his finger in the chocolate dough, then ate a clump of it.

"Stop," Alice scolded. "That's raw dough."

"I eat raw cookie dough," Harry said. "What's wrong with brownie dough?" He stuck his finger out and gave me a taste.

"If you eat all the dough, you won't have any brownies," Alice said. "Now keep stirring."

She pulled me out of the kitchen, into the little office she had across the hall. "Harry really likes you," she confided in a whisper. "He's been talking about you a lot."

"Nice," I said. Alice had a smear of chocolate on her

cheek. I pointed it out to her. She rubbed it away with two fingers.

"Brownies can be messy with an eight-year-old chef," she said. "Anyway, I think you made a big hit with Harry on Monday."

I felt a chill at the back of my neck. I suddenly pictured the demon-creature running across the landing at the top of the stairs. Harry hiding in the front hall coat closet . . .

"Did Harry say anything about . . . about . . ." I hesitated. "About anything weird happening?"

Alice squinted at me. "Weird? No. He just said he had fun."

"My hand hurts. How long do I have to stir this?" Harry shouted from the kitchen.

"I'll be right there," Alice called.

I had this sudden urge to confide in her. Tell her everything that happened that first night at Harry's house.

Would she understand?

Of course not. She would tell Brenda I was crazy. She would warn Brenda not to use me anymore. I realized I had to keep it to myself.

But what if it happened again? What if the intruder appeared in the house again?

No. No way.

"I'm glad Harry likes me," I told Alice. "I like him, too. He's pretty special."

Alice promised to bake the brownies and have them ready

for Harry the next day. I walked him home as raindrops began to patter down.

My heart began to race as we stepped into the house. My eyes immediately went to the top of the stairs. In the kitchen, I began to warm up the dinner Brenda had prepared for Harry. Every creak, every scrape, every soft sound made my muscles tense.

I was on super-alert.

Even Harry noticed I was tense. "What's wrong, Lisa?" he asked as he ate his early dinner. "You look kind of worried."

"No. I'm fine," I lied. "Just thinking about . . . school."

After dessert, I asked Harry if Alice had given him homework.

"I don't think so," he replied. He scratched his dark hair. "I don't remember."

I laughed. "You're a liar. Of *course* you remember."

He tickled me under my chin. Somehow he had discovered I'm very ticklish there. "Lisa, I'll tickle you until you let me play with my Xbox," he threatened.

I had no choice. I had to give in. He likes to play a game called *Candy Catastrophe* endlessly. I watched for a while, but it got to be boring. "Don't you have any other game you like?" I demanded. "How can you play this for a solid hour?"

"I like it," he said, eyes on the screen as the colored candy pieces tumbled.

"But is that your only game?"

He shook his head. "Mom bought me a monster game. But I don't like it. Too scary."

A monster game?

I shuddered. Pictured the demon-creature again. Saw its ugly, twisted face as it looked up at me from the backyard.

My phone beeped. I picked it up. A text from Saralynn: *Everything ok?*

I texted her back: *Fine. No problem.*

I saw that my phone was practically out of power. I didn't have my charger. "Does your mom have an iPhone charger?" I asked Harry.

He shrugged. "I don't know."

I let him play a few more rounds. Then I tucked him into bed early. He went without an argument. No pleas to stay up late tonight. I guessed he was sleepy.

Rain pattered the bedroom window. I made sure it was closed. I checked his closet. No sign of any demons.

The evening had gone fine. No problems at all. But I couldn't relax.

I sat down on the living room couch and pulled the science assignment from my backpack. It was interesting reading, about how a new strain of bees had appeared, aggressive bees that liked to attack, and no one knew how this type of bee had suddenly developed.

Frightening.

Regular bees were scary enough.

The article told about a man who was stung on the face

by six of these bees and died instantly. When my phone rang, I jumped and uttered a startled cry.

I fumbled for it, picked it up, and read the caller ID:

Summer Lawson.

27.

I stared at the screen with the phone poised in my hand. I didn't answer, just let it go to voicemail.

What does she want? What is her problem?

I waited a few seconds, then checked. She didn't leave a message.

I tossed the phone down and went back to the killer bees. They were known to attack dogs and even raccoons. Scientists were studying their genetic makeup.

I don't know why, but I've always found insects fascinating. I guess it's because there's lots more insects than humans on the planet. It's *their* planet and we don't really know that much about them.

I finished the article and went back to highlight some sections. I like to read a whole piece first, then go back and underline what I think is important.

I glanced at the front window. The rain had stopped but the window was still covered in raindrops. Moonlight trying to get through the window was broken into a thousand little shiny pieces.

I sucked in my breath when I heard a sound. A soft *thud*.

In the kitchen?

I jumped off the couch. My whole body tensed as I stood there, fists at my sides, listening.

I heard the creak of a footstep. A scraping sound. Another creak.

Someone was definitely in the kitchen. I wasn't imagining it. Someone had broken into the house and was creeping through the kitchen, trying to be quiet, coming toward the living room—coming for me.

The same intruder? The same monstrous creature?

I was frozen there. Not breathing. I don't think my heart was beating. It was as if I'd turn to an ice sculpture. I felt cold all over, the cold tingling of total fear.

I didn't think I could move.

There. Another footstep. A soft cough. Closer.

My phone. I dove for it. My hand trembled so hard, I nearly dropped it.

Got to call 911. Please—let me call 911 before he comes bursting in.

No. Please—no.

The phone was out of power. Dead. The screen wouldn't even light up.

No phone. And another footstep.

Who's there?

I tried to call out those words, but no sound escaped my open mouth.

I squeezed the dead phone in my hand, squeezed it so hard my hand throbbed with pain.

On trembling legs I made my way to the hall. Still not breathing. Not breathing. Somehow I made it to the kitchen door.

The floor seemed to tilt and sway beneath me. The whole world was spinning.

But I forced myself to the kitchen. Holding onto the door frame, I leaned into the room. Gazed all around—and then cried out in total surprise.

28.

What are *you* doing here?" I choked out.

I stared at Nate, standing on the other side of the white kitchen counter.

He wore a black denim jacket zipped to the top. The shoulders were wet, and his hair was matted to his forehead. He'd obviously been out in the rain.

He gave me a weak smile. "I rang the front doorbell. Didn't you hear it?"

"No," I said. I was still trembling. My heart was still doing flip-flops in my chest. "No, I didn't. I was in the living room, but I didn't hear the front door."

"Maybe the bell is broken," he said, stepping around the counter. He kept his brown eyes on mine, a smile frozen on his face. "When you didn't answer, I came around the back."

I sucked in a deep shuddering breath. I realized I was hugging myself, trying to calm myself.

Nate stepped up to me. His smile faded. He put a hurt

expression on his face. "Aren't you glad to see me?" He reached out to hug me, but I pushed him back.

"Y-you scared me to death!" I stammered. "Seriously. I thought someone broke in."

He snickered. "Someone *did* break in. Me."

"You're not funny," I said. "Why didn't you say something? Why didn't you call me first? Why didn't you—"

He put a hand over my mouth. "I wanted to surprise you, that's all."

I shoved his hand away. "I hate surprises. You weren't trying to scare me—were you?"

"No way," he said. "I wouldn't do that."

"Then why are you here?" I demanded. I started to feel calmer. I stopped shaking. I realized I was actually glad to see him.

He brushed back his wet hair. "I was driving past. I have to go pick up my brother. He's at a friend's house a few blocks from here. It's like a full-time job, driving Tim around. But I thought I'd just peek in and see if you were okay."

I laughed. "I was okay until you frightened me to death."

He stepped forward and kissed me on the cheek. "Sorry," he said softly. "I didn't mean to. Really. I just remembered you were upset after last Monday. . . ."

His voice trailed off. I knew he didn't believe me about what I saw here on Monday night.

"Well . . . I guess it was sweet of you," I said. "Can you come back and pick me up after Brenda gets home?"

"No problem." He pointed to a plate on the counter. "Are those chocolate chip cookies homemade?"

I opened my mouth to answer, but I heard a shout from upstairs. "That's Harry," I said. "See you later."

I spun away, trotted across the living room, and started up the staircase.

"Lisa! Hey, Lisa!" Harry's cries were shrill. He sounded frightened.

"I'm coming," I called as I reached the second-floor landing.

I pushed open Harry's door. The room was totally black, as usual. I fumbled on the wall till I found the light switch and clicked on the ceiling light.

He was sitting straight up in his bed in his *X-Men* pajamas, his face red, his eyes wide. "Lisa—I . . . I was scared. I heard voices."

I crossed the room and dropped down beside him. "That was just my friend, Nate," I said. "He stopped by. No reason to be scared."

He stared at me as if trying to decide if I was telling the truth. His chin was trembling. I leaned forward and hugged him. "Settle down. Get back under the covers. Everything is fine," I said.

He scooted down and I tucked the quilt under his chin. "Goodnight," he said in a tiny voice.

"Goodnight, Harry. I'll be right downstairs if you need anything. Don't worry. Go to sleep, okay? It's very late."

"Very late? Can I stay up? Can I stay up late?"

"No. No way," I said. "You're already half-asleep."

He nodded and shut his eyes. I gazed for a moment at his cute face, his blond hair spread out on the pillow. Then I hurried downstairs to scold Nate for scaring the kid.

"Nate? Hey, Nate?" I crossed the living room, into the back hall to the kitchen. "Did you leave?"

He wasn't in the kitchen. I noticed a few cookies were missing from the plate. I didn't hear him leave, but I guessed that Nate had gone to pick up his brother.

I returned to the living room and picked up my phone from where I'd tossed it onto the couch. I made a mental note to remember to bring a charger with me from now on.

I settled on the couch and reached for my backpack. I had more homework to do, but I didn't remember what it was. I thought about Nate creeping through the kitchen. Why didn't he knock on the kitchen door before he came in? Why didn't he call out as soon as he entered the house?

He probably was afraid he might wake up Harry.

I leaned forward and started to paw through the books and other junk in my backpack. But I sat straight up when I heard a sound. The soft squeak of a floorboard. My breath caught in my throat.

"Nate? Is that you?"

My voice came out in a hoarse whisper.

Silence.

And then I heard shallow breathing. A rhythmic wheezing. Close to my ears.

I spun around. "Nate? Are you back?"

No one there.

Panic gripped the back of my neck. I suddenly felt cold all over. "Who's there? I can hear you. Nate? Harry? Did you come downstairs?"

No reply. The breathing grew more rapid, each breath sending a chill down my back.

And then I gasped as a blur of motion across the room caught my eye.

And the backpack fell to the floor as I jumped to my feet—and gaped in silent horror at the demon-creature, hunched at the bottom of the stairs.

29.

This isn't happening. Please—tell me I'm hallucinating.

I wasn't. I stood frozen, my fists tight at my sides.

We had a staring contest. He had one huge hand resting on the banister. He was normal height, not very short or very tall. His legs were spread, as if ready to run.

His eyes were red as burning coals, surrounded by the tight greenish reptile skin that covered his face. He had green pig ears that poked up from the top of his head. His animal snout hung open, revealing two rows of pointed teeth.

Wheezing loudly, his chest rising up and down, he took a lumbering step away from the stairs. He walked unsteadily, like an animal not used to standing on its two feet. Grunting sounds came from deep in his throat.

"Who are you?" I screamed in a shrill voice I didn't recognize. "What do you *want?*"

He lurched forward another few steps. He didn't reply.

Does he speak? Does he understand English?

Crazy questions. But your mind goes crazy when you are terrified beyond anything you've ever felt.

"Stay away!" I screamed. "Go away!"

He took another heavy step toward me. Then he tilted his fur-topped head back, uttered a shrill hissing sound, puckered his black lips, and spit a huge gray-green gob of gunk into the air. It shot across the room and landed with a loud wet *splat* on the coffee table at my feet.

I screamed and forced myself to move. I darted to the back of the couch. Another thick gob of spit landed on the couch-back in front of me. It sizzled as it sank into the cushion.

"Nooooooo!" I let out a long wail as I watched the creature raise both arms as if preparing to grab me. I spun away from behind the couch. My eyes shot back and forth, looking for an escape route.

Another snakelike hiss from the creature. He snapped his jaws, making his pointed teeth click. Again. Again. The clicking sound hurt my ears, like chalk squeaking on a chalkboard.

Panting in terror, I watched as he sent another wad of spit flying toward me. I ducked, and it sailed over my head and made an ugly *splat* sound on the wall.

I stood up—and uttered a cry as the next disgusting wad of spit hit me, stunned me, splattered over my hair and forehead. The warm gunk oozed down my face. It smelled putrid, like rotten eggs.

I raised a hand to wipe it away. And now my hand was

covered in sticky goo. I stood there, unable to decide what to do, the spit sinking into my hair, running down my face.

And then . . . something inside me snapped. I felt a weird burst of energy. A wave of anger swept over me. *"Stop! Go away!"* I shrieked. *"Go awaaaaay!"*

I must have temporarily lost my mind. Because instead of backing away from the ugly, spitting creature, instead of trying to escape, I pushed myself forward. I lurched away from the wall—and went after him.

I lowered my head like a football running back and went charging at him.

The creature's red eyes flared. The hissing stopped. He turned and took off, staggering away from me toward the front door.

Roaring like a wild beast, I flew after him.

He turned at the doorway, ducked past me, and trotted back into the living room. He had a strange, twisted grin on his black lips, as if he was enjoying the chase.

He stopped at the side of the couch. Leaped onto the coffee table. Turned and waited for me to come after him.

But I ran to the stairway. I was panting hard, my face burning hot and stained with sweat. I wasn't thinking clearly. I didn't have a plan. I knew only that I wanted to protect Harry. I wouldn't let the creature go up the stairs again.

We had another staring contest. The creature perched on the coffee table, big gnarly hands on his waist. For the first time, I noticed that he was dressed in baggy brown clothes, a long shirt that came down nearly to his knees. Brown leggings revealing bare, fur-covered feet at the bottoms.

A horror-movie creature that wore clothes?

The insanity of it made him even more frightening to me. He had to be real. If I had imagined him, I'd never put him in clothes. . . .

More crazy thoughts.

My whole body tingled with cold sweat as I struggled to catch my breath.

And then the creature was moving again. Grunting loudly, he ran straight to the wall. Hoisted himself onto the dark-wood bookcase. Then scrambled straight up. To my shock, he ran up the wall. *Then ran across the ceiling!* His large bare feet slapped the ceiling as he ran upside-down across it.

He spun and dropped into the hall. His feet thudded the floor as he plunged into the kitchen. I heard the kitchen door slam hard.

Did that mean he was gone? Did he run out of the house?

I hunched with my hands pressed over my knees. I stayed there, my chest throbbing, hair falling over my sweat-drenched face, gasping for air.

When I could finally move, I pushed my hair off my face, took a deep breath, and strode to the kitchen. I stopped at the doorway.

A chill tingled my neck as I realized it could be a trap. The demon-creature slammed the door to make me think he had left. But he was lurking there, waiting to trap me.

I hesitated. Then, one hand on the doorframe, I leaned forward and peered into the kitchen. No one there. He was gone.

I let out a long breath. My chest still ached from our insane chase.

Now I had only one thought in my head. Harry. Was Harry okay?

I hurried to the stairway. I started to take the stairs two at a time.

I was halfway up the steps when I heard the scream.

A shrill scream of horror. A girl's scream. From outside? Right outside the house?

I stopped. And heard a second scream, high and desperate. A frantic scream for help.

I turned to the front door.

What is happening out there? Who is screaming like that?

30.

I stumbled and nearly toppled off the steps. The screams sent chill after chill down my back. Someone right outside the house was in horrible trouble.

The demon-creature had run out the back door. Had he attacked someone in the front of the house?

A horrifying thought made me gasp. *Was that Brenda screaming?*

Harry's mom, home from work. She climbs out of the car. And the creature leaps on her.

"No," I whispered. "Please—no."

I tore down the stairs and ran to the front window. The front porch light sent a cone of yellow light over the front yard. I saw tall weeds swaying in a breeze. The grass gleamed silvery under the light.

No one there.

I ran to the front door and tugged it open.

Silence now. The shrill chirp of crickets. The whir of the grass and weeds blown by the swirling wind.

"Anyone out there?" My voice sounded muffled, choked by my fear. "Hello? Anyone there?"

A gust of wind blew my hair back. I waited. And listened. No one there.

I pushed the door closed. The chill of the night air lingered on my skin. Once again, I heard the shrill shrieks and cries in my mind.

I didn't imagine them.

I pressed my back against the front door and gazed at the stairway. It took me a few seconds to realize I'd forgotten about Harry. Was he okay? Did he hear the screams? Did he sleep through my chase around the living room with that ugly creature?

I took a deep breath. My mouth was dry as cotton. My legs were trembling. But I forced my way up the stairs. The floor creaked under my shoes as I hurried down the long hall.

I stopped outside Harry's door. I reminded myself to pretend to be calm, nonchalant. I remembered how frightened Harry was the first time the creature appeared.

I grabbed the knob and slowly pulled the door open. So dark in there. The darkness seemed to creep out through the open doorway, to spill out into the hall.

"Harry?" I whispered.

Blue light washed into the room from the open bedroom window. The curtains flapped wildly in the strong breezes.

My eyes slowly adjusted to the darkness. I made my way

on tiptoe to the side of Harry's bed. I could hear his soft breathing.

He was lying on his side, facing me. His eyes were shut tight. His mouth was open slightly. His hair was spread over the pillow.

He slept through everything.

I let out a sigh of relief. I watched him sleep for a few more seconds. Then I crept over to the window and closed it, and made my way out of his bedroom.

Back in the living room, I couldn't sit down. I paced back and forth, clenching and unclenching my fists. I thought about calling my mother and telling her the whole frightening story about the demon-creature. But I knew what she'd say. She'd say I was hallucinating again, that I wasn't ready to take on this babysitting job.

Should I call 911?

The police wouldn't believe me, either. Why should they believe such a crazy story? They'd think it was some kind of prank, some kind of high school dare.

I had to tell someone. Who could I turn to? Before I could decide, I heard the back door open. Footsteps clicked across the kitchen floor.

The creature has returned.

That was my first terrifying thought. I froze in place, my eyes on the back hall.

When Brenda walked into the room, I nearly collapsed from relief.

She set her pocketbook and briefcase down and turned to me. "Lisa? Are you okay?"

"Well—" I started. But a voice from the stairway interrupted.

"Hi, Mom."

I turned to see Harry halfway down the stairs.

Brenda's mouth dropped open. "Harry? Are you still awake?"

A pleased smile spread over his face. "I stayed up late."

"That's terrible!" Brenda exclaimed, her eyes on me.

"That's not true!" I cried. "I was just in your room, Harry. You were sound asleep."

His smile grew wider. "I was pretending."

"But—why?" I said. "I don't understand." I turned to Brenda. "I put him to bed at eight o'clock. I—"

"Never mind," Brenda said wearily. Her tiredness showed on her face. "Harry, go back to your room. I'll come up in a few minutes and tuck you in."

He turned without another word and half-jumped, half-ran up the stairs.

"He needs his sleep," Brenda said, unbuttoning her suit jacket. "He's terrible if he stays up late."

"I had no idea he was awake," I told her. I made sure Harry wasn't still on the stairs. Then I whispered, "Brenda, I have to talk to you."

She motioned to the couch and we both sat down. My heart started to race. I knew I couldn't hold it in any longer. I had to tell her about the frightening intruder in the house.

Would she believe me? Would she think me insane or something?

"I have to tell you something," I said softly. "Something serious."

She narrowed her eyes at me. She grabbed my hand. "Lisa, you're trembling. What is it you want to tell me?"

31.

The long blast of a car horn made me jump. It was so loud, I thought it was inside the house. It took me a moment to realize it was Nate in the driveway.

"Who's that?" Brenda climbed to her feet.

"It's my friend Nate. He came to pick me up," I said.

Brenda glanced to the front window. "Will he wait? Do you want to invite him to come in?"

Another blaring horn blast. "N-no," I stammered. "I think I have to go. Next time—"

"Well, what did you want to tell me?" Brenda demanded. "Is it about Harry? Is he misbehaving?"

"Not at all," I said, gathering up my backpack. "Harry is an angel. Totally. We can talk when I come back. I—"

She followed me to the front door. "No. Wait, Lisa. Tell me what you wanted to talk about. I won't let you leave till you tell me."

"Well . . ." I knew I should tell her. But I didn't want to just blurt it out. I didn't want to sound like an insane person, seeing monsters in the living room. "I just wanted to ask if you have an iPhone charger," I said. "My phone went dead tonight and—"

"No problem," Brenda said. She pulled open the front door for me. Cool air rushed into the front entryway. "I'll leave one out for you next time." She shook her head. "I thought you had something serious to tell me."

I forced a laugh. "Well, a dead phone is pretty serious." She smiled. I said goodnight and hurried out to the driveway.

I stepped up to the driver's side of the car and tapped on the window. Nate slid it down halfway. "Why are you being so impatient?" I asked.

He started to answer, but I interrupted. "Hey—what are those scratches all over your face?"

He rubbed his cheek. "You won't believe how clumsy I am," he said. He winced and put his hand down. "I went to pick up my brother at his friend's house, and would you believe I fell right into a rose bush? There were like dozens of thorns. My face is killing me."

"Are you serious?" I said. "You got those deep scratches from rosebushes? That's hard to believe. Whoa. Look. You have some dried blood by your ear."

"That's why I'm in a hurry to get home," he said. "Come on. Get in."

I started around the back of the car to get into the passenger seat. But I stopped when something caught my eye on the ground across the street. Something on the curb in front of the empty lot.

I squinted into the dim light. "Hey, Nate—" I called into the car. "Come with me. There's something weird across the street."

He frowned out at me. "I'd really like to get home, Lisa. My face—"

But I jerked open his door and tugged him out of the car.

We were nearly to the bottom of the driveway when I saw clearly that it was a body lying in the curb.

A human body.

I sucked in a deep breath. Nate and I stepped up to it, walking side by side. "Oh, nooooo." A long moan escaped my throat. I covered my eyes. "A girl!" I cried. "Nate— it's a girl."

"I don't believe this." His voice came out in a muffled whisper. "She—she's been clawed up. I mean, clawed to pieces."

I opened my eyes. The girl's clothes were ripped open. And . . . and . . . her stomach was ripped open, too. Her guts spilled out onto the pavement. And were those *bite marks* up and down her body?"

"No. It can't be. It can't be." The words gushed from my throat. "No. No way."

And then my eyes slowly traveled up to the girl's face. And I recognized her.

Summer Lawson.

PART
FOUR

32.

The walls of the little square room were a sick vomit green and the paint was peeling near the ceiling. Two lights hung from the ceiling inside gray cones. One of the bulbs was out.

It was Tuesday morning, the morning after we found Summer's body. We sat on folding chairs around a long table, the top covered in names and initials that people had carved into the wood. The room smelled of stale cigarette smoke despite the stenciled NO SMOKING sign tacked to the wall.

Of course, I was tense. I'd never been interviewed by a police officer before. I kept clasping and unclasping my soggy hands under the tabletop and clearing my throat.

My mother sat a little behind me to my right and kept petting my shoulder with her good hand. Guess she was tense, too.

Nate sat across from us. He wore a white short-sleeved

shirt over dark khakis. First time I'd ever seen him not in jeans.

"Are those your dress-up clothes?" I asked, my voice sounding too loud in the tiny, windowless room.

He nodded. He kept his eyes down. He kept scratching his hair, brushing it back, then forward.

Sam Goodman, Nate's father wore a navy blue suit, a pale blue shirt, and a dark bow tie. His head is shaved. He's very pale. And he wears thick black plastic-framed glasses that slide halfway down his nose. I think he looks like a lightbulb with glasses, but he's very nice. He was busily texting on his phone as we waited for someone to come in and talk to us.

"Hot in here," Mom murmured. She shifted her cast uncomfortably.

"There's no ventilation at all," Mr. Goodman said, raising his eyes from his phone.

"The police like to sweat confessions out of people," I said. I was trying to make a joke, but no one laughed.

Finally, the door swung open and a tall officer in a starched black uniform, gold badge tilted on his shirt pocket, stepped in. "Sorry to keep you waiting," he said in a hoarse, gravelly voice. "I'm Captain Rivera."

Rivera was in his thirties, probably. He was tall and wiry except for his belly, which stretched the front of his uniform shirt. His black hair was shaved close to his head. His face was tanned. He had a broad forehead, tiny, serious black eyes set deep, and a carefully brushed black mustache that curved down the sides of his mouth.

He pulled a folding chair up to the end of the table and dropped into it. He placed an iPad on the tabletop and tapped a few things on the screen. "I'm going to record this meeting," he explained. "You know. So we can all be sure of what was said."

The four of us watched him without saying a word. Mom stopped petting my shoulder and settled back on her chair. Mr. Goodman slipped his phone into his suit jacket pocket.

"Let's go around the table and say your name and age," Rivera said. "For the record." His eyes were on me. He chuckled. "Don't look so frightened, Lisa," he said. "We're all friends here."

I could feel myself blushing. "I'm just a little stressed," I said. "I mean, I can't stop picturing . . ." My voice trailed off.

"Lisa has some emotional issues," Mom chimed in.

"I can't stop picturing Summer's body," I said, glaring angrily at my mother. "I saw a dead body, Mom. That girl was murdered. It has nothing to do with my emotions."

Rivera motioned with one hand. "Let's all try to be as calm as we can," he said. "If we can continue . . ."

We took turns giving our names and ages. For some reason Mom said she was thirty-nine. I know for a fact she's forty-two. She stared at me as if challenging me to correct her.

"You and Nate are our first eyewitnesses," Rivera said, pushing the iPad to the center of the table. "You were the first ones at the murder scene." He rubbed his chin. "It must have been horrible for you."

I nodded. "I . . . still see her lying there. I can't get the picture out of my mind."

"It was an unusually gruesome murder," Rivera said. "I'm sure you've heard what the media is calling it. The Cannibal Killing."

Silence. Then Nate's dad spoke up. "So, it's true? Whoever did this to the girl . . . did they really *eat* parts of her?"

My throat tightened. I suddenly felt like I was about to lose my breakfast.

Rivera frowned. "I know you two saw the bite marks on Summer Lawson's body. Well, our lab guys say they are from human teeth. And parts of the torn-off flesh . . . well . . . a lot of flesh was missing . . . skin and meat and bones. It wasn't at the scene. She was torn apart and eaten."

"But no human could do that," Mr. Goodman said, his voice cracking.

"Right," Rivera agreed. "No human could do that—or would want to. But the bite marks—they were human."

He turned to me. "You were there, Lisa. You were at Brenda Hart's house all evening. Can you tell me what you saw and heard?"

I cleared my throat. I clasped my hands over the tabletop. "Well . . . I didn't see anything," I started. "I heard screams. Frightening screams. Right outside the house. Like a girl screaming for help."

"Did you recognize who it was? Did you recognize it was Summer Lawson?"

I shook my head. "No. I . . . I couldn't tell. I was on the front stairs. I stopped and listened. She screamed twice. The second scream—it was cut off."

Rivera toyed with the badge on his pocket. "And what did you do? Did you run outside to investigate?"

"No," I said. "I ran to the front door and I looked out. But I didn't see anything at all. And the screams had stopped."

"So what did you do next?" Rivera asked, his dark eyes locked on mine.

"I hurried upstairs. To make sure Harry was okay. I mean, that was my job. To make sure he was all right."

"And was he all right?"

I nodded. "Yes. He was in his bed."

Rivera frowned. "So you didn't see the body until Nate arrived to pick you up."

"Yes," I repeated.

"And did you see anything suspicious at all? Anyone on the street? Anyone who was outside or walking by or anything at all that caught your eye?"

"No," I said. "No one. It was ten o'clock at night and—"

"Go ahead, Lisa. Tell him," Mom interrupted. She

squeezed my hand. "Don't hold back. Tell him about the creature you say you saw."

"Creature?" Mr. Goodman said, blinking behind his black eyeglasses. "Nate didn't say anything about a creature."

Rivera leaned over the table as if to get closer to me. "What kind of creature? What did you see?"

My stomach suddenly felt like a rock. A wave of dread swept down my body. I took a breath.

"Some kind of creature appeared in the house," I started. "It . . . it was the second time I saw it. He walked on two legs like a man. But his face was all twisted and ugly. Kind of green-tinted. With pointed teeth and huge pig ears poking up from a strip of fur on his head."

I saw the shock on Mr. Goodman's face. His mouth dropped open. His eyes bulged.

Nate avoided my gaze. He kept his head lowered.

"It started to attack me," I continued. "But I turned on it and chased it. It ran up the wall and across the ceiling, and—"

"It ran upside-down on the ceiling?" Rivera interrupted.

"Yes. I chased it out of the house. I was so frightened. Then a minute or two later, I heard the screams."

Rivera squinted at me. "And you thought . . . ?"

"I couldn't think. I was so terrified. I couldn't think straight. I was shaking. I could barely breathe. Later, I put it together. I figured the creature I saw had attacked Summer . . . had killed her."

I gripped the edge of the table. My hands were wet and ice cold. The room was silent. I kept my gaze on Captain Rivera.

Does he believe me? DOES he?

33.

Across the table, Nate and his father stared at me. Their faces had no expression at all.

I turned away from them and waited for Captain Rivera to react. Silently, I begged him to believe my story.

He rubbed his fingers down his mustache, his eyes trained on me. Finally, he spoke: "This was a movie you saw?"

I let out a long sigh.

"Not a movie," I replied through gritted teeth.

"You fell asleep and had a nightmare about chasing a creature around the house?"

"I was wide awake, Captain Rivera," I said, unable to hide my anger, my disappointment that he wouldn't believe me. "I saw what I saw and—"

My mother squeezed my arm. "Lisa and I were in a terrible car crash," she interrupted. "Lisa had a very bad concussion."

"Sorry to hear that," Rivera murmured, studying me.

"I'm afraid ever since the accident, Lisa has been seeing

things," Mom continued, biting the lipstick on her bottom lip. "She is working with a very good doctor, but . . ." Tears rolled down her cheeks.

Rivera was silent for a long moment, rubbing two fingers down his mustache.

I felt about to burst from frustration. Whose side was she on?

"Mom, please—give me a break. The creature was real," I cried. "I wasn't *seeing* things. I didn't dream it. It had flaming red eyes. It had pointed teeth that looked like they could rip apart human flesh."

"Like some kind of comic-book demon?" Rivera said.

He didn't give me a chance to answer. He turned his gaze on Nate, who hadn't said a word. "Nate, you told us you were in the house earlier that night."

Nate nodded. "Yes, I was there. I dropped in to see how Lisa was doing."

"And did you see any funny-looking monster in the house?" Rivera asked.

"No," Nate replied.

"Did you see a monster running across the ceiling?"

"No, I didn't."

"It showed up right after Nate left," I said, my voice shrill and angry. "Nate didn't see it. I was the only one to see it. But that doesn't mean—"

Rivera raised a hand to silence me. He kept his attention on Nate. "Later, when you and Lisa discovered Summer's body, did you see some kind of creature running around the front yard? Or maybe running down the street?"

"No," Nate replied softly.

Rivera nodded, a thoughtful expression on his face. He studied me for a long moment. "Do any of you have anything else to add?" he said finally. "Any detail that might help my guys? Any little thing you saw?"

"I can't remember anything else," Nate said. "I . . . I've never seen a dead body before. I mean . . ." He lowered his head. He still refused to look me in the eye.

He thinks I'm crazy.

They all do.

Captain Rivera stood up. "I'm giving you all my card," he said. "It has my direct line on the back. If you think of anything at all, call me immediately."

He opened the door and stood aside so we could leave. "Thank you all for coming in," he said. He stopped me as I passed him. "Lisa, I hope your concussion gets better. Brain trauma can really be frightening."

34.

Later, I paced back and forth in my room. I crossed my arms in front of me as I walked. Then I lowered them and clenched and unclenched my fists.

I didn't know what to do with myself. I wanted to jump out of my skin and fly away. Escape. I didn't want to be me. I didn't want to be someone everyone thought was crazy, someone everyone felt sorry for.

Saralynn called but I didn't answer. She texted me: *Where r u?*

I didn't answer her text. I was beginning to suspect she wasn't a very good friend. Why were she and Nate together so often? I had a strong feeling something was going on between them.

I didn't have any real proof. I just had a hunch. A strong hunch.

I desperately wanted someone to confide in. Someone to believe me. But I could picture the fake sympathetic expression on Saralynn's face if I told her about the demon-creature. I could hear her telling me I should discuss it with my doctor.

Who *could* I confide in?

Mom was hopeless. Nate wouldn't even look me in the eye when we sat right across from each other at the police station. Could I talk to Isaac about it? No way.

So many questions whirred through my mind as I paced my room, I could feel the blood pulsing at my temples. I never get headaches but now I could feel the pressure building, and my forehead felt ready to explode.

Why was Summer Lawson outside Brenda Hart's house that night?

She was coming to see me. She wanted to warn me about Nate.

But—what *about* Nate? I realized I really didn't know him that well. I mean, I was really attracted to him. And he seemed to care about me.

So what did Summer want to tell me?

Unless . . . unless . . . *Did it have something to do with his horror collection?*

No way.

Sure, Nate has all those masks and movie posters and props from old horror films. But *lots* of people are into horror.

Nate collects that stuff for fun. It doesn't mean he is into *real-life* horror. It doesn't mean he secretly wants to be a crazed ax murderer or carry a chainsaw around.

That's a totally insane idea.

So what did Summer want to warn me about? What was *wrong* with Nate?

When I asked him point-blank, he made a joke about it. He said she was jealous, that's all. He said she was crazy.

I flung myself facedown on the bed. Tears were forming in my eyes, but I forced myself not to cry. "What a mess," I muttered to myself. "What a total mess."

No way I wanted to go back to that house on Fear Street. *No way* I wanted to risk seeing the creature again or pass the spot across the street where Summer was murdered. And *eaten.*

But did I have a choice? Mom and I had no money. Mom couldn't go back to work because of her arm. I needed to keep the job. I had to go back there. And to be honest, I felt close to Harry. I didn't want to abandon him.

Who could I talk to? Who? I never felt so alone.

Of course, Dr. Shein was the logical person. She was kind and caring. She would listen. She would be understanding. But she was a doctor. She wouldn't believe that the demon-creature was real.

I couldn't confide in her, even though that's why I kept going to see her. I didn't want to be put on medication. I didn't want to be treated like a sick person. I knew I wasn't sick. This was *really happening.*

And then a face floated into my mind. The face of someone I knew would believe me. The face of someone who always took me seriously. The only person I could confide in.

"I miss you, Dad," I whispered into my pillow. "I miss you *so much*."

Wednesday morning, I pulled Nate out of study hall, and we sneaked outside. It was a warm spring day. The sun was high in a cloudless blue sky. The air smelled fresh and sweet.

I held his hand and tugged him across the student parking lot at the back of the high school. I recognized Isaac's green Honda, a guitar standing up in the backseat. The bike rack was filled and several bikes were on their sides, strewn on the ground around it.

"Where are you taking me?" Nate asked. We both kept looking back to the school to see if anyone had seen us.

"*Sshhh*." I put a finger on his lips. I pulled him to the far side of the parking lot behind a tall SUV. "I want to talk to you."

He brushed back his hair and smiled. Then he slid his arms around my waist and pulled me close. "We should be in study hall. This is dangerous. But I *like* dangerous."

He kissed me, softly at first, then the pressure of his lips hardened and his mouth opened.

"No," I pulled my head back. "I want to talk. Seriously."

He laughed and kissed me again, holding me tightly against him so I couldn't escape. I returned the kiss. I really did like him. But then I squirmed out of his grasp.

We were both breathing hard. I grabbed him by the arms and pushed him back. "You don't understand, Nate. I have to talk to you. I'm desperate."

His smile faded. His dark eyes locked on mine. "Talk?"

I could still taste his lips on mine. "I don't have anyone else I can talk to," I said. "I need you to believe me."

"About the creature you saw in the house?"

I nodded. "Yes. It was real—not in my mind. I didn't imagine it, Nate."

He frowned. "You know I'm into horror, Lisa. Horror movies and games and stuff. But it's hard to believe—"

"People warned me about Fear Street," I said. "About the evil things that happen there. Don't you think it's possible—"

He shook his head. "Lisa, you've been imagining creatures since the accident."

I felt a burst of anger. "I didn't imagine Summer being murdered—*did* I?"

He took my hand. "I'm sorry," he murmured. "You're very upset."

"I'm beyond upset, Nate. I'm . . . I'm . . ." I didn't know what to say.

"You have to chill," Nate said, squeezing my hand. "That's all you can do. You know Dr. Shein said your subconscious is playing tricks on you."

I nodded. "Yes, she did," I said in a whisper.

But then I tugged my hand free. I took a step back.

WAIT a minute, I thought. *I don't remember telling Nate what Dr. Shein said.*

How does HE know what my doctor said?

I realized I was staring at the scratches down Nate's face. A chill tightened the back of my neck.

Summer wanted to warn me about Nate, and now Summer was dead.

And Nate's face had those long scratches down both cheeks. From a rosebush? Really?

Nate is all scratched. Summer is dead.

Am I *next*?

35.

Should I be afraid of Nate?

That's crazy, I decided. My mind is going crazy. Nate is just Nate.

I realized I was still breathing hard. If only I could push away these crazy thoughts. I must have told him about Dr. Shein. And those scratches really could have been made by walking into a rosebush in the dark.

"Nate," I said, "I really need you to believe me. I need you to—"

"Can I ask you a question?" he interrupted. He brushed a fly away from his face. I couldn't read his expression. He narrowed his dark eyes at me.

"Sure," I said.

"What's up with you and Isaac?"

"Huh?" The question startled me. And he asked it like an accusation.

"You and Isaac," he said. "I saw you kiss him."

I couldn't help myself. I laughed. "Have you been holding that question in all this time?"

"It isn't funny," he said. "Are you and Isaac—"

"No," I said. "That was nothing. You don't have to think about that." I gave him a playful shove. "Don't be dumb. I don't have a thing about Isaac. Anyway, I thought we were talking about me and my babysitting job."

He nodded. "Okay. Okay. Let's drop it." He glanced over my shoulder to the school. No one there. No one had seen us.

"I really don't want to go back to that house," I said. "I know you don't believe me, but that creature is real. What if he decides to kill me next?"

Nate scratched his head. "You can't just quit and never go back there?"

"Mom and I need the money. Brenda is paying me three-hundred dollars a week."

"*Phew.*" Nate whistled. "Big bucks. *I'll* take the job!"

"Don't be funny," I said. "I need you to be serious. I—"

He squeezed my hand. "I have an idea. A good idea."

"Well? Spill," I said.

"I can't come tonight. But I'll come with you Friday," he said. "I'll stay with you the whole time. Will that make you feel safer?"

"Hmmmm." I thought about it. "That's a sweet offer," I said finally. "Really. But I don't think Brenda would approve if I have my boyfriend over. I mean, I'm supposed to pay all my attention to Harry."

He blinked. "Okay. Okay. No worries. Here's a better idea. What if I bring Saralynn, too? Brenda shouldn't have a problem if all three of us are there to entertain Harry."

"Well . . ."

Nate and Saralynn again. They were practically inseparable. Was I being paranoid? Was something going on, or did Nate just want to help me?

I saw a flash of color by the side of the school building. I turned and, squinting into the sunlight, I saw Saralynn against the brick wall. She wore a bright red top, which caught my eye.

"Did you know Saralynn is over there?" I said, pointing.

Nate turned. His face filled with surprise. "No way. How did she know we were out here?" He motioned to her, and she came trotting toward us, her long hair floating up behind her.

"Hey," she said breathlessly. "Are you two hiding back here? Third period is almost over."

"We were just talking," I said.

She studied me. "You okay?"

"Not really," I said.

"I have a good idea," Nate said.

"That's a first!" she joked. She gave him a playful shove. He pushed her away.

"No. Seriously," Nate insisted. "Lisa is afraid to go back to the house on Fear Street. So I said you and I would stay with her Friday night. You know. Help entertain the kid."

"And help entertain me," I added.

Saralynn didn't even think about it. "Brilliant!" she exclaimed. She tossed her hair back with a wave of her head. "Count me in."

She flashed Nate a knowing look.

Saralynn didn't even think about the plan for Friday. It's as if she already knew about it.

She and Nate keep exchanging glances, like something is up between them.

"That will be awesome," Saralynn said to me. "And we'll keep you from getting freaked. Can we order a pizza?"

I started to answer, but I heard the class bell ring inside the building. "We'd better get back," I said. "If someone catches us out here . . ."

We started across the parking lot toward the back door. Saralynn and Nate walked fast. I started to trot, trying to stay up with them.

They were both talking at once, their heads close to each other.

I was pretty far behind them, but Saralynn's voice carried on the wind. And I was sure I heard her say:

"Shouldn't we just *tell* her the truth?"

Did I really hear that?

What did she mean? The truth? The truth about what?

36.

After school, I hurried to Alice's house. The TV was on in the den, but Harry wasn't there. I found him on his stomach on the living room rug, reading a picture book about spiders. He raised his head with a big smile when I came in. "Lisa—hi!"

He was so glad to see me. It made me instantly feel more confident.

Harry wore a red-and-blue striped polo shirt and navy shorts. His legs were skinny and pale and looked like toothpicks stuck in his red sneakers.

"Are you afraid of spiders?" he asked.

I leaned over the book. The photo on the page was so closeup, it made the spider look as big as a cat. "I'm definitely scared of *that* big dude," I said.

That made him laugh.

I heard footsteps on the stairs and Alice appeared from the basement. She was carrying a large wooden salad bowl and looked surprised to see me. "Lisa? Are you early?"

"No. I came right after school." I heard the human-sounding cat cry from the basement.

She bumped the basement door closed. "I've been running behind all day."

"Look at this red spider," Harry said, stabbing the book with his pointer finger. "That's a scary one."

"The red color sure makes it look angry, doesn't it," I said. "Are you ready to go home? Maybe you could take the book home, and we both could look at it there."

"Could I see you for a moment?" Alice said. I detected tension in her voice. She motioned with her head to the kitchen.

I followed her. She set the big salad bowl down on the counter and blew a strand of hair off her forehead. She looked more tired than usual, her eyes kind of dead, deep circles around them.

"Harry is enjoying that spider book," I said. "Maybe he'll be a scientist when he grows up."

"He says he doesn't like scary things. But he *devours* anything about bugs or snakes," Alice said. She wore a long plaid shirt over faded jeans.

"Did you study spiders today?" I asked.

She didn't answer. She stepped up close to me. "I want to talk to you seriously," she said, lowering her voice. She glanced back to make sure Harry hadn't followed us.

I had a sudden feeling of dread. "Is anything wrong?" I asked.

"You let him stay up late on Monday, didn't you?" she

said. "It's very bad for him. It's important you get him to sleep at the right hour."

I swallowed. "Actually, I put him to bed a little after eight," I said. "I think he stayed up late without me knowing it. He came out on the stairs when Brenda came home. He was bragging about how he stayed up late. But I didn't know—"

"You have to make sure he goes to sleep," Alice whispered, glancing to the kitchen door again.

"Why?" I said. "Does Harry need more sleep than other kids his age?"

Alice nodded. She jammed her hands into her jeans pocket. I heard the cat cry again from downstairs, a sad wail.

"Brenda doesn't like to admit it. But he has a condition," Alice said. "It has to do with brain patterns. I'm not a doctor. I think it's something like epilepsy. If he has his sleep, he's fine. Perfectly normal. He needs a regular sleep pattern to regulate these brain patterns."

I didn't really understand, but I nodded.

"If he doesn't get his regular sleep," Alice continued, "he's a very different kid, very difficult. It makes him moody, even angry. But his personality definitely changes, and he totally loses his ability to concentrate." She sighed. "Those days are difficult for me, being his teacher. And there is always the possibility of seizures."

"Seizures? Really? I-I-I'll be more careful," I stammered. "I didn't know. Brenda didn't tell me. She only said—"

"Brenda has a lot on her mind, what with the new job

183

and all. That's why I'm so happy to be able to help her out."
She smiled. "Also, because I love Harry so much. He's really an angel. And as I said, he really is perfectly fine . . . if
he gets his sleep."

"Yes, he's terrific," I said.

And there he was at the kitchen door, the spider book
tucked under his arm. "Lisa, can we go home now?"

I wanted to ask Alice about last Monday night. Had
Harry heard anything about the murder across the street?
Had he heard the intruder in the house? The frightening
chase I had with the ugly creature?

"Come on, Lisa," he pleaded, grabbing my hand and tugging me to the kitchen door. "I want to go home. Can we
play *Candy Catastrophe* tonight?"

"Maybe after you do your homework," I said.

He grinned at me. "My homework is *Candy Catastrophe*."

Alice and I both laughed. "What about the arithmetic
worksheet?" Alice said.

Harry shrugged. "Maybe I forgot it."

I walked him home. I really didn't want to go into that
house again. I wanted to stay at Alice's where it was pretty
and quiet and comfortable, and there were no creatures
lurking.

But what choice did I have?

I took a deep breath as I unlocked the kitchen door and
vowed to be brave. Alert and brave. I'd checked my phone
after school to make sure it was fully powered. If there was
any trouble tonight, at least I'd be able to call for help.

Harry and I paged through the spider book for a while. Then I made dinner for the two of us. Brenda had left a package of ground beef, and I made hamburgers. I kept them on the stove a little too long, but Harry didn't seem to notice.

I kept listening for any sound, any blur of movement. My senses were on super-alert, but I was determined not to give Harry a clue that anything might be wrong.

It was obvious that he didn't know about Summer's murder across the street. That made me very relieved. He was such a sensitive kid. If he heard anything about it, I knew he'd be totally freaked.

He begged to stay up late. But I told him firmly he was going to sleep on time tonight. He made a pouty face, sticking out his bottom lip. It made me laugh, and he started to laugh, too.

I tucked him in at exactly eight o'clock with a stern command to go right to sleep. He yawned. I could see he was tired. *He shouldn't be a problem tonight,* I thought.

Downstairs by myself, I kind of wished I'd kept Harry with me. The house was silent except for the hum of the fridge in the kitchen and the *click click click* of the clock on the mantel. The silence made me even more tense, more alert.

I took out my phone and plugged in the earbuds. Maybe some music would help distract me from the horrible silence. But then I thought better of it, and tucked the phone back into my bag. I needed to stay alert.

Sitting stiffly on the couch, my eyes kept darting to the stairway, expecting the ugly creature to be hunched there again. I'd finished my homework. I had nothing to do. I needed something to entertain me.

I called Saralynn but it went right to voicemail. I picked up the spider picture book and riffled through it. It wasn't any fun without Harry to ooh and ahh over every creepy spider.

"I should quit this job," I murmured to myself. *It's too dangerous,* I thought. *It's crazy to stay here. The creature is real, and he's already killed someone.*

I jumped to my feet and started to pace, as if trying to escape my frightening thoughts. I hugged myself as I walked back and forth. Pale moonlight washed in from the living room window. Outside, all was as still as death. Not a leaf moved, no tree branch swayed, no car headlights swept over Fear Street.

Maybe the stories about this street are true.

I stopped pacing and gazed at the bookshelves against the back wall. A stack of white albums caught my eye. I stepped closer and saw that they were photo albums.

I'm not a snoop but I needed something to do. I pulled the top photo album off the shelf and carried it to the couch.

Curious, I spread it open on my lap. The first page held a large wedding photo. Brenda and the guy she married. What happened to him? When did they split up? I wondered. He was a good-looking guy, very clean-cut, very all-American, tanned, blue-eyed, short brown hair, a nice smile.

I turned a few pages. There was baby Harry. He was only a few months old and he already had curly blond hair. Photos of Brenda and husband playing with the baby. An outdoor photo of the three of them in a park, walking Harry in a stroller.

A few pages later, I stopped at a large photo of a crowded picnic. Blankets spread on the grass. Picnic baskets. Kids throwing a Frisbee. A family reunion, maybe. No sign of the husband. I spotted Brenda sitting cross-legged in the grass, a Coke bottle raised in one hand.

And then on the next page, a posed picture from the picnic. Everyone huddled in a group, grinning at the camera, kids sitting on the grass, adults behind them.

And . . . wait.

My mouth dropped open as I stared at the face in the middle row on the far right.

No. That's impossible.

Nate?

Yes. Nate's face. Nate, maybe a few years younger, standing with his arm around a girl in a red sweater.

"Oh, wow," I muttered, my heart starting to thump in my chest. "That's Saralynn."

Yes. Saralynn. Her hair shorter. Saralynn and Nate grinning at the camera.

But how could this be?

Why were Saralynn and Nate in Brenda's photo album?

37.

I gazed at the photo for a long moment. Were my eyes playing tricks on me? No. Saralynn and Nate grinned out at me from the family picnic scene.

Brenda stood on the other side of the group, with one hand resting on Harry's head. Harry had a plastic sand shovel in one hand. One of his knees had a big bandage on it.

I turned the page, hoping to find other photos with Saralynn and Nate. But the next page had photos of Harry on a school playground. In one shot, he was hanging upside down on a jungle gym. Brenda stood in the background, hands on hips, looking very tense. I guess she didn't like to see him hanging like that.

I shuffled quickly through the rest of the album. But my two friends didn't appear again.

My two friends? Really?

My head spinning, I shut the album and returned it to its place on the bookshelf.

Why were the two of them there? Why? I had to find out.

I tried phoning Nate first. The phone rang and rang and didn't go to voicemail. I tried Saralynn again, and again her phone went directly to voicemail.

"Call me," I said. "I have a question."

Then I dropped onto the couch, pressed the back of my head against the cushion, and tried to figure out what I'd just seen.

Brenda returned home a little before ten. "Everything okay?" she asked, dropping her briefcase on the floor and hurrying over to me. Her face was tight with worry.

"Very quiet tonight," I said. "I got Harry to sleep early. He was tired."

She dropped onto the couch beside me. "Lisa, I'm so sorry about what happened here Monday. I've been worried about you all day. After . . . after Monday, I thought maybe you wouldn't want to come back."

"Well . . ." I started. "I was a little afraid—"

"You must have been terrified," she said. "Something so horrible happening right across the street. Were you scared tonight?" She answered her own question. "Of course you were. I'm scared to be here, too."

"Well, I kept expecting—" I started again. But again she interrupted me, her dark eyes wide with concern.

"I hope you'll stay on the job, Lisa. I know you must be tempted to get as far away from here as you can. But I hope you'll stay for Harry's sake. He's quite fond of you already. Really. He talks about you all the time. Even though you haven't been here long. . . ."

"I'm fond of him, too," I said. "He's a very sweet kid. And he makes me laugh."

I suddenly realized how attached to Harry I was. I really did care about the kid. And I wanted to protect him.

"So you'll stay?" Brenda asked.

"Okay," I said softly.

She smiled and patted my arm. "I'm so glad."

I opened my mouth to ask her about the photo album. I was desperate to know about that picnic photo. But I realized Brenda would think I was snooping. Not a good idea to tell her I was going through her photo album. So I said goodnight and headed for home.

I didn't get any answers until I finally reached Saralynn a little after midnight. "Where were you?" I whispered into the phone.

My mom thought I had gone to sleep at eleven. But I'd been trying to reach either Nate or Saralynn for the past hour.

She groaned. "I had to go to my cousin's house. She lives so far out of town, my phone had no bars. Would you believe I'm just starting my chem homework? I'm going to be up all night."

"I have to ask you something," I said. "You have to tell me the answer. I'm going crazy."

"I'll try," she said. Then she remembered where I was tonight. "Hey, how'd it go at Harry's house? Everything okay?"

"Yeah, no problem. But I was tense the whole time. Like my stomach was tied in a tight knot."

"I'd be totally freaked," Saralynn said. "I mean, I wasn't there, but I still can't stop thinking about poor Summer. You know, they're having grief counselors in school tomorrow if you want to talk to someone about it."

"I just want you to answer one question," I said.

"Shoot."

"I didn't have anything to do, so I was looking through one of Brenda's photo albums. And there was this photo of you and Nate at a big family picnic."

Silence for a moment. Then, Saralynn spoke slowly: "Uh . . . yeah. I know."

"What were you two doing there?" I asked. "I mean, I was so totally shocked."

Another silence. Like she was thinking hard, trying to decide how to answer.

"I *told* Nate we should tell you," she said finally. "I don't know why he was acting so weird about it."

"Weird about what?" I demanded. "What did you want to tell me?"

"Nate and I are related to Brenda," Saralynn said. "The three of us . . . we're like second cousins or something."

I blinked. My brain was trying to download this information. "I don't understand," I said finally. "You and Nate and Brenda are all cousins? Why did you want to keep that a secret?"

"I didn't want to keep it a secret," Saralynn replied. "It wasn't my idea. But Nate . . . I couldn't get Nate to explain. Sometimes he's just weird about family things."

"Weird?" My head was spinning. "I don't get it. I really don't."

That explains why Nate and Saralynn seem so close, I told myself. *They don't have crushes on each other or anything like that. They're cousins.*

"That picnic photo must have been a surprise," Saralynn said.

"Uh . . . yeah," I said. "You have me all confused, Saralynn. I thought I could trust Nate. Now I'm not sure. Why would he keep that secret from me? And we are friends. Why didn't *you* tell me?"

"I kept pleading with him to tell you. But he said something about confusing you. He didn't make any sense."

"Maybe you and Nate shouldn't come to Brenda's house Friday night," I said. "I don't really want you there if I can't trust you."

"Can't trust us? That's harsh."

"I'm sorry," I said. "I didn't mean to sound that way. But—"

"We really do want to help you," Saralynn said. "We care about you. I can't explain about Nate. But we want to be there for you."

She sounded sincere. I felt bad that I had snapped at her. But I felt so bewildered by Nate keeping that secret. It didn't make any sense at all.

What other secrets does Nate have?

"Isaac wants to come Friday night, too," Saralynn said.

"He said he'd come to Brenda's right after his band practice."

"Well . . ." I said.

"We're your friends, Lisa. Let us help you," Saralynn
pleaded.

"Okay, I guess," I relented.

"Awesome," she said. "It'll be like a party. We'll have
fun, and we'll take care of Harry, and we'll make you feel
safe."

"Okay," I repeated. But I still had a heavy feeling of dread
tightening my throat.

I hope I'm not making a big mistake.

38.

Friday afternoon, I picked Harry up at Alice's. Harry had his backpack all packed and appeared eager to go as soon as I showed up.

"Where's Alice?" I asked.

"In the basement," he said and pointed to the door that led to the basement. "Can we have mac and cheese tonight?"

"No problem," I said.

"And can I stay up late?"

"No way, Harry." I brushed his hair off his forehead. His blond hair was so curly and awesome, it was hard to keep your hands off it. To tell the truth, I was totally jealous of his hair. Mine is straight and thin and I never know what to do with it.

Alice appeared from the basement, her face in a tight scowl. When she saw me, she forced a smile. But I could see that she was tense and tired.

"Tough day?" I asked.

She walked to the fridge and pulled out a bottle of water. "No. Just the same old same old." She took a long drink.

"Lisa says I can have mac and cheese," Harry told her.

Alice squinted at him. "I made that for you for lunch."

He shrugged. "So?"

I laughed. Alice didn't seem amused. She rolled her eyes and took another long drink of water. She waved us to the door. "Go," she said. "Have fun. But, Harry—don't forget you have to practice your cursive tonight."

He nodded. "First I have to play my Xbox game."

Alice turned to me. "Make him practice his handwriting. He writes like a gorilla. Brenda can't even read his *printing*."

"*Oooofoooofoooof*." Harry made gorilla grunts and scratched his armpits like a monkey.

Normally, Alice would have laughed. But today she just let out another long sigh and waved us to the kitchen door again.

I took Harry home and made him practice his handwriting first thing. Then I made him his precious mac and cheese and we both had an early dinner.

"Can I stay up late if I promise not to tell Mom?" he asked in his sweetest, tiniest voice.

"No way," I told him. "My friends are coming by tonight. We need to study. We have a big test coming up."

He made a disgusted face and spat a macaroni noodle across the table at me. "You're very rude," I said.

"But I'm cute," was his reply.

Nate and Saralynn showed up together a little after six thirty. Harry was glad to see them. He gave them both hugs. Nate picked him up and swung him around. I realized they'd known Harry his whole life.

I felt a stab of anger, anger at Nate for keeping that secret. But I forced it away.

Nate studied me. "Everything back to normal?" he asked.

I nodded. "So far, so good."

Saralynn stood over the table and finished the macaroni left on Harry's plate. "Do you have mac and cheese for breakfast, too?" she asked Harry.

"Sometimes," he said. He grinned. "And sometimes for a snack."

We all played his *Candy Catastrophe* game for a while. I could see that Saralynn and Nate were letting him win.

A little before eight, I powered the game off. Everybody booed. "Be quiet," I said. "Harry has to be in bed by eight. That's the rules."

To my surprise, he jumped up and ran to the stairs without even saying goodnight to Nate and Saralynn. He didn't seem sleepy, but he changed into his SpongeBob pajamas and let me tuck him in without a word of complaint.

When I returned downstairs, Saralynn was on the floor playing *Candy Catastrophe* with the sound muted. Nate leaned forward on the couch, his thumbs moving over his phone keyboard.

"Isaac's band rehearsal must be running late," he told me. "He said he'd be here by now."

I dropped down next to him on the couch. He slid an arm around my shoulder and pulled me close. We kissed, but I ended it quickly. "I have to talk to you," I said.

He leaned back. He glanced at his phone. No reply from Isaac. He turned back to me. "This was a good idea, right? Our coming over to keep you company?"

"Sure. Fine," I said. "It's not what I want to talk about. Why didn't you tell me that you and Saralynn are Brenda's cousins?"

Saralynn glanced up from her game, as if she was eager to hear Nate's answer, too.

He wrinkled his nose. Then he shrugged. "I . . . well . . . I didn't want to interfere in your job."

I narrowed my eyes at him. He was trying to act casual, but he twitched his nose again, and he kept picking at a callus on the palm of his hand.

"Does that make any sense at all?" I said. "I don't think so."

Nate shrugged. "Sorry. Guess I was wrong. I just didn't think it mattered."

I shook my head. *He still isn't making any sense. Something is missing here.*

I studied him. He looked so uncomfortable. He lowered his eyes to his phone.

"You should have told me," I said. "I really don't see the issue here. Why would I care that you're related?"

"Sorry," he muttered.

"Should we do some prep for the chem final?" Saralynn

suggested. She turned off the Xbox. "I'm kind of freaked about it. I mean, I didn't exactly keep the workbook up to date."

"Mine is a disaster," I said. "Because I missed those weeks of school."

"You can share mine," Nate said. He pawed through his backpack, found the notebook, and tossed it to Saralynn.

We studied for about an hour, sometimes together, sometimes on our own. It was about a quarter to ten when Nate jumped up. "When is Brenda getting home?"

"She's going to be late tonight," I said. "Maybe eleven. Where are you going?"

He was halfway to the front door. "Isaac didn't answer my texts. He should be here by now."

"You're going to find him?" Saralynn asked.

He nodded. "I'm going to run over to his house and see what's up with him. I'll be back in a few minutes. Try not to miss me *too* much."

He disappeared into the front entryway. I heard the front door slam behind him.

"Does he seem tense to you?" I asked Saralynn.

She turned the page in the chem notebook. "He seems like Nate. You never know what you're going to get."

I squinted at her. "I guess I don't know him very well. I mean, we've only been going out for a month. Is he . . . moody?"

"Sometimes," she answered. "It's not like he's got a mental problem or anything. I mean, sometimes he's more up than other times. Nothing to worry about. He just gets in different moods."

I nodded. We studied in silence for a while. Then I thought of something else. "Did you finish that horror video you were doing in Nate's backyard?"

She shook her head. "No. It sucked. I mean it was totally lame. I'm in major trouble. I have to think of a new project before the semester is up."

I shook my head. "Whoa. That's a drag. Do you have any ideas?"

Saralynn started to answer.

But my scream cut her off.

Gazing to the top of the stairs, I saw him. The demon-creature. He had his long fingers curled around the banister. He was leaning toward us. His red eyes were glowing. His green-tinted skin caught the light from the ceiling. His snout was open in a toothy grin.

I screamed again. And pointed with a trembling hand.

Saralynn squirmed around to face the direction I pointed. "Lisa? What's wrong? What do you see?"

"He's there!" I choked out. "The creature. At the top of the stairs!"

Her eyes went wide. She started to breathe in short, hard bursts.

"He's watching us!" I screamed. "He's watching us!"

Her face twisted in confusion, Saralynn turned back to me. She grabbed my hand. "Lisa," she said. "There's nothing up there."

39.

The creature curled and uncurled his snakelike fingers around the banister. Under the bright ceiling light, his green head gleamed. The eyes darkened to purple embers.

"Saralynn—look at it!" I shrieked. "At the top of the stairs! Look at him staring at us!"

She squeezed my hand. She tried to wrap me in a hug, but I leaped to my feet.

"Lisa—I don't see anything," she said. She stood up, too. And stepped away from the couch, striding toward the stairs. "Where?" she demanded. "Where do you see it?"

On the top step, the creature tossed back his head, his mouth wide in silent laughter. He bent his knees and slapped the banister with both hands. Enjoying himself. Enjoying my terror and confusion.

"Saralynn—don't you see it? I . . . I'm not imagining it. He's standing there. He's laughing at us."

"Lisa—there's no one on the stairs."

"Ohmigod. Ohmigod. You don't see him? Really? Ohmigod." My voice sank to a harsh rasp. "Is he really just in my head? Am I really crazy?"

Saralynn spun away from the stairway. She reached out her arms and pulled me into a tight hug. My body was trembling so hard, I thought I would fall. I felt my knees start to give way.

"Lisa, *ssshhhh,*" she whispered. "Try to calm down. Lisa, try to stop shaking. It's okay. We're safe. There's no one up there."

"But—but—" I sputtered.

She pressed her cheek against mine and whispered in my ear. "Should I call your doctor?"

"N-no," I stammered. "I—"

"She might make you feel better," Saralynn insisted. "She might give you something to calm you down." She loosened her hug and took a step back. Her chin trembled. "This must be so horrible for you, Lisa. Please—tell me what I can do to help."

I took a deep breath and held it, trying to stop my body from shuddering. I turned from her and gazed back to the top of the stairs. No creature.

"Harry," I murmured. "Harry is up there. I've got to make sure Harry is safe."

Once again, I pictured the ugly demon-creature running across Harry's room, leaping out the window, scrabbling over the backyard grass.

I forced my legs to move and took off. I ran up the stairs. Saralynn was close behind.

My shoes thudded the carpet as I led the way down the long hall. I grabbed the knob, shoved open the door—and burst into the room.

Silver moonlight washed in from the open window. I turned to the bed. The covers were pushed down.

Harry was gone.

40.

Saralynn stared at the open window. "No!" she let out a whispered cry. "Harry didn't jump out. He wouldn't."

"No," I said. "He's hiding. Like last time." My heart was pounding so hard, I could hear the blood whistling at my temples. "Like last time," I repeated.

"Where?" Saralynn demanded. "Where did he hide?"

I didn't answer. I ran back downstairs. To the front hall. I tugged open the coat closet door. "Harry, it's okay," I said. "You can come out."

I gasped when I realized he wasn't in the closet.

"This is where he hid?" Saralynn leaned into the closet, shoving coats out of the way. No sign of him.

"He-he's in the house somewhere," I stammered. "He gets frightened and—"

"I'll search upstairs," she said. She turned me around by the shoulders. "You search down here. Search every closet. Every room. We'll find him. I know we will."

"But . . . what frightened him?" The question just blurted

from my mouth. I didn't even think of it. "Saralynn, stop. If you didn't see the creature . . . If there was no creature . . . what frightened Harry?"

"It had to be your screams," she answered. "Lisa, you screamed so loud. Your screams were so terrifying . . . they frightened *me*!"

"You're right," I murmured. "Yes, you're right. I frightened Harry. Come on. Let's find the poor guy and let him know he is safe."

She went running back up the stairs. I crossed the living room into the back hall. I searched the kitchen pantries and under the table. "Harry? Harry?" I cupped my hands around my mouth and shouted his name over and over.

I searched the maid's room in back. Cardboard cartons were stacked to the ceiling in the tiny room. "Harry? Are you here?" No.

I pulled open the doors to two other closets in the back hall. Then I returned to the living room. I glanced all around. My head was spinning. No. The whole room was spinning. Panic gripped my chest, tightened all my muscles.

"Harry? Can you hear me? Please come out."

I heard Saralynn slam a bedroom door upstairs. I heard her shoes on the hallway floor.

I decided to join her up there. I was nearly to the stairs when I heard a sharp noise outside. A hard bump. Like some kind of collision.

I stopped. And listened. Totally alert. Not breathing.

I heard shouts. Scrabbling sounds. A hard *thud*.

A fight? Two people fighting in the front yard?

A sharp grunt. Another *thud*.

I didn't think. I pulled open the front door and stepped out under the harsh glare of the porch light.

I squinted down the front yard toward Fear Street. At first, I didn't see anything. Just the tall grass swaying slightly in a soft breeze.

But the *hissss* made me spin toward the driveway. A hiss like a dozen snakes all attacking at once.

And then a scream. A hideous painful scream. A scream that didn't stop. It seemed to ring in my ears forever. Frozen there in panic on the porch, I instantly knew I would never forget this scream. Never be able to erase it from my ears.

And then I saw the creature lope away, half-trot, half-stagger toward the darkness of the street. I saw it. And I heard it grunt . . . grunt with panting breaths as it staggered away.

"Nooooooo." A long, horrified moan burst from deep inside me as I saw the body, a heap on the grass near the driveway.

I turned back to the house. Where was Saralynn? Still upstairs?

And then my legs carried me . . . Against my will, my legs carried me over the grass, wet with evening dew, over the soft swaying grass toward the heap on the ground.

I stopped a few feet away. My stomach lurched. I slapped my hand over my mouth to keep from puking. Pressed both hands over my mouth and stared at the mutilated body.

Isaac.

Yes. Isaac.

His eyes stared up at me, wide and blank and shiny as glass. His mouth hung open, locked in a silent scream.

His T-shirt was ripped down the front. His stomach was torn open, the skin split right down the middle. His intestines, pink in the moonlight . . . half-eaten . . . half-*eaten* . . . like sausage links . . . spilled onto the grass.

41.

Where were you when Lisa discovered the body?"
Captain Rivera had his arms crossed in front of
him, his eyes on Nate.

We were back in the little, windowless room at the Shadyside precinct house. Sitting tense around the table. Once
again, my mother hunched on a folding chair behind me.
Across the table were Nate and Saralynn and their fathers.
Captain Rivera perched restlessly at his end of the table, a
paper container of coffee, an iPad, and a writing pad in front
of him.

Across from him, a woman officer. I think her name was
Clemens. She had short, dark hair brushed straight back,
tiny black eyes over a stub of a nose. She grimaced and
scowled as if she didn't want to be there. She kept fiddling
with the cuffs of her black uniform shirt.

"I wasn't there," Nate answered. His voice cracked, and
he cleared his throat. "I was in my car. Driving around.

Trying to find Isaac." Nate kept scratching his face and twitching his nose. He seemed really tense.

The room was hot. There was no air-conditioning. Nate had large beads of sweat glistening on his forehead.

"Where did you look for him?" Rivera asked.

"Uh . . . well . . . I started at his house," Nate said. "He wasn't there. He was supposed to come join us after his band practice. But practice was over, I guess. No one was at his house."

"So then what did you do?" Rivera asked.

"Drove around the block a few times," Nate replied, wiping sweat off his forehead with the sleeve of his T-shirt. "I drove past the school. Looking for his car. I didn't know if he was walking or driving."

Rivera typed something on the iPad. "So you weren't near Brenda Hart's house at around ten thirty? You were still driving around, searching for your friend?"

Nate nodded. "Yes. That's right."

Rivera turned his gaze to Officer Clemens. "Did the coroner send over a time of death?"

She shook her head. "Still working on it. He said it had to be between nine and ten thirty."

"Saralynn, let me ask you the same question," Rivera said, stroking his mustache with the palm of his hand. "Where were you when Lisa discovered the body? Were you still in the house?"

Saralynn had tear stains on her cheeks. She had been crying nonstop all morning. She said she hadn't slept for one second last night after I found Isaac in the grass.

I'd never known her to be so emotional. But, of course, I didn't know her that well. And this was an extreme situation.

That morning, I asked myself why I didn't cry. I decided I was in some kind of shock. I didn't want to believe any of this was happening. Actually, I told myself I'd be happy if it was all another hallucination, all my own nightmare, or just happening in my poor, broken mind.

Weird thoughts.

But who wouldn't have weird thoughts after finding two people you know torn to pieces?

"Yes, I was in the house," Saralynn said. "I didn't know Lisa went outside. I was upstairs, looking for Harry."

"The little boy," Rivera said. "And where did you find Harry?"

"He was hiding," Saralynn said. "Hiding in a closet in a guest room. He said he heard shouts that scared him."

Rivera narrowed his eyes at Saralynn. "He heard shouts? Inside the house or outside the house?"

Saralynn hesitated. "I . . . don't know. Maybe he heard Lisa screaming."

"I screamed when I saw something at the top of the stairs," I offered.

"I know," Rivera said, frowning. "We'll get to that in a minute." He motioned to Saralynn. "Go on. What about

Harry? He heard shouts, so he hid in a closet? Like the last murder, am I right?"

"I don't know," Saralynn said. "I wasn't there last time." She wiped tears off her cheeks with a tissue. "We knew Harry was freaked last night. We didn't tell him there was a murder. But he was very upset. We had to call the police, and I guess he overheard us. And he kind of lost it."

Rivera blinked. "Lost it?"

"Started crying and screaming he wanted his mom," I chimed in. "He knew something was very wrong. He could see how upset Saralynn and I were. So he became very frightened."

"We did everything we could to calm him down," Saralynn added. "And we didn't tell him what happened outside. He just picked up the vibe, I guess."

"He has a condition," I told Rivera. "He's not supposed to stay up late. It messes up his brain circuits or something. His mom is angry at me for letting him stay up last night. But Saralynn and I were downstairs. We didn't even know he was still awake."

Rivera typed some more on the iPad. His fingers were stubby, and he kept making mistakes. He sighed. "Okay, I guess we have no choice," he said, turning to me. "I guess we have to discuss this creature thing. But I'm warning you, Lisa—"

"I saw it at the top of the stairs," I insisted. "I swear. That's why I screamed."

Officer Clemens leaned forward. "What are we talking about here?" she asked.

"Some kind of creature," I said, my voice shaking. My heart was pounding. I knew they didn't want to believe me. "He walks on two feet. He looks like a man. Except his face is twisted and ugly, like a demon. And—"

"Like a demon in a horror movie?" Rivera interrupted. "Do you watch a lot of horror movies, Lisa?"

His question was hostile. He was accusing me of hallucinating the thing. But I knew I'd seen it. I knew. At least, I was pretty sure. . . .

"I don't like horror movies," I replied. "Ask Nate. Nate is a horror freak."

Rivera turned to Nate. "Is that true? Did you see a horror-movie demon in Brenda Hart's house?"

Nate shook his head. "No. Lisa says she saw it after I left the house to go look for Isaac."

"I can describe him totally," I insisted. "I'm not making him up. His skin is tinted greenish, a light green. He has red eyes that appear to glow, sunk deep in his face. His head is bald except for a strip of thick black fur in the middle of his scalp. His ears are pointed and stand straight up."

My voice broke. I wanted so desperately to be believed. "I couldn't make that up, Captain Rivera," I said. "I don't have that good of an imagination."

"Oh, I think you do," Rivera said.

It was a stinging comment, meant to hurt me. And it did.

Rivera didn't let up. He leaned closer to me. "You've had some mental problems, is that right?"

"Mental problems?" My voice broke. "No. Not really. I—"

"You've had bad nightmares. You've seen things that weren't there?"

"She's working with a doctor," my mom chimed in.

"Mom—*stay out of it!*" I shrieked. I realized immediately I shouldn't have yelled like that.

I have to act calm. I can't give them any reason to think I'm crazy or unbalanced.

Rivera's eyes burned into mine. "Lisa, did you have some kind of nightmare in which you were angry at Summer and Isaac? Did you maybe have a dream that you attacked them?"

I uttered a loud gasp. "Are you *accusing* me?" I cried. "Do you think I could have murdered those kids?" My heart was drumming so hard, I could barely get the words out.

"Do we need to get a lawyer?" my mom asked Rivera.

He raised both hands. "I'm not accusing your daughter. I have to ask every question." He leaned forward again. "Lisa, this demon-creature you say you saw . . . Was it YOU? Is it possible that you created this monster because you couldn't face what *you* did to Summer and Isaac?"

A hush fell over the room. It was like time had stopped. All eyes were on me. No one even blinked.

My whole body went rigid. I forced myself to breathe.

And then a scream burst out of me from deep in my throat. "*Noooo!* I'm not crazy and I'm not a murderer!"

My mother jumped to her feet. "Lisa and I are leaving," she told Rivera through gritted teeth. "We don't have to sit here and—"

Rivera waved her back down. "I'm sorry. I am not trying to upset you. But a boy and girl have been brutally murdered. They were your friends. And you are the only one who seems to know who killed them."

"No. Wait," I choked out. "I didn't say—"

"You tell me it's some kind of monster," Rivera interrupted. "I'm sorry. I can't accept that, Lisa. I need you to tell me the truth. Why won't you tell me what you *really* saw?"

"But I *did*!" I insisted.

Silence now. He kept his eyes narrowed on me, studying me. Waiting for me to say more.

He thinks I'm an insane murderer.

A sob escaped my throat. My mother squeezed my hand.

Rivera sighed and brushed a hand back over his shaved head. Finally, he turned his gaze from me. "Saralynn," he said, "you were in the living room with Lisa when she looked up the staircase and screamed. Did you see the creature, too?"

Saralynn, tears in her eyes, silently mouthed words across the table to me: "I'm sorry."

She wiped the tears with one finger. "Lisa pointed to the top of the stairs," she said softly. "She was screaming. I mean, she was in a total panic. But I didn't see anything up there."

"Did you see a shadow or something?" Clemens chimed in. "Something that might resemble a figure up there?"

Saralynn shook her head. "No. Nothing. Lisa kept screaming and pointing. Telling me the creature was up there looking down on us. But . . . but the stairs were empty. I didn't see anything. Not anything. I felt so bad for her."

She turned to me. "I'm so sorry, Lisa. But there wasn't anyone up there. I'm so sorry."

I didn't react. I didn't reply. It was like my brain froze. I suddenly felt numb. Totally numb all over.

Rivera asked Saralynn a few more questions. But I didn't hear their conversation. I saw Saralynn's mouth moving, but I couldn't hear the words.

I had a loud whistling in my ears. The sound of my brain freezing, I guess. I didn't even try to hear what they were saying.

I can't tell you how frightening it is to have your friends and everyone else think you are crazy. And maybe even a deranged murderer. It's frightening and frustrating and makes it impossible to think clearly or act normally, or act at all.

When the question session was over, and we were all out on the street, Nate and Saralynn hugged me and then disappeared as quickly as they could, along with their parents.

I was left standing there in the precinct parking lot with my mom. Still numb. Still hearing that shrill whistling in my ears. Still lost in my jumbled thoughts, wondering what really happened last night.

And I turned to Mom and tugged at her good arm. "I n-need to see Doctor Shein," I stammered. "I think . . . I think I really need her help. Saralynn was there with me. She didn't see the creature. But I saw it so clearly, as if it was real. What's *wrong* with me?"

42.

Dr. Shein chewed the eraser on her pencil. Behind her, rain pattered the window. She had a vase of yellow lilies on the corner of her desk, and the sweet aroma washed over the office, so strong it made my eyes water.

She listened in silence as I sat in the red leather armchair across from her and told my sad story. Her face remained expressionless. Behind her glasses, her eyes trained on me. She didn't blink.

As I talked, I watched the raindrops slide slowly down the window. Like teardrops, I thought. The patter of the rain . . . the ticking clock on her glass desk . . . the hoarse sound of my voice as I relived the horrifying night . . . Those were the only sounds.

And when I stopped talking—silence.

Dr. Shein chewed at her eraser. Her gaze rose over my shoulders. She seemed to disappear into herself, as if she were fading into her thoughts. Even her aqua top under her cream-colored jacket appeared to lose its glow.

When she finally set down the pencil, brushed back her hair, and spoke, her words weren't what I expected to hear. "Lisa," she said, "I thought you would be further along by now."

The words stung. I don't think she meant to startle me or upset me. But I expected something a little warmer, a little more encouraging.

She leaned forward. "It's understandable," she said. "These horrible murders of your friends . . . they are agitating you even more. And I'm afraid we're left with one difficult question."

I clasped my hands together tightly. Where was she going with this?

"The question is, what can we do to make these hallucinations stop?"

I swallowed. My mouth suddenly felt as dry as cotton.

Dr. Shein fingered the locket on her chest. "You know I want to try everything I can to make you better, to make sure you return to functioning normally."

I rubbed my damp hands on the knees of my jeans. "But what if I really saw some kind of monster?"

Dr. Shein shook her head. "Stop thinking like that, Lisa. Your friend Saralynn was there. She didn't see anything, did she? If it was real, wouldn't she have seen it, too? You don't really believe that you have a special power, do you? That you can see monsters other people can't see?"

"No—" I started. "But . . ."

"Let me explain what's happening, dear," she said, softening her tone. "Let me tell you what your brain is doing."

I settled back on the armchair. I took a deep breath to relax, but I couldn't force away the tension that tightened all my muscles. "Okay," I said in a voice just above a whisper. "Please—tell me."

Dr. Shein shut her eyes for a moment, gathering her thoughts. "You suffered a terrible loss," she started. "Your father. You lost your father in an accident caused by human error. Your mind doesn't want to face that, Lisa. Do you see where I'm going?"

I nodded. "I think so."

"Your mind doesn't want to face the truth," she continued. "You'd rather think that some kind of monster was responsible for the awful things that happened."

I thought about it for a long moment. I understood what she was saying. But I couldn't agree. "What about Summer?" I said. "What about Isaac? They were torn apart. Their bodies were ripped open. Parts of them were *eaten*. Don't you think a monster—?"

She shook her head. "Think about it, Lisa. Once again, you want to replace a human with some kind of demon. The truth is, an evil *human* killed your friends. A very sick and dangerous person was responsible. But it was a *person*. Your mind wants to create a fantasy that—"

"You mean I'm crazy?" I cried. "Is that what you're

trying to say? I slip into a fantasy world and I don't know what's real and what's only in my imagination?"

I gripped the chair arms. My nails dug into the leather. I gritted my teeth hard and tried to stop my body from trembling.

Dr. Shein motioned with one hand for me to calm down. "Take a breath, Lisa," she said softly. "Take a deep breath and let it out slowly. I didn't say you were crazy, dear. You have to listen more carefully. I'm sorry if my explanation is upsetting. But we can deal with this. And we *will* deal with this . . . together."

I eyed her suspiciously. "What do you mean?"

Again, she motioned with one hand. "Sit back. You're all tense. Let yourself breathe."

I followed her instructions. I pressed myself against the chair back. I unclasped my hands.

"I'm going to prescribe some meds to calm you down," she said. "And I have a medication in mind that will work as a gentle mood elevator."

I stared at her, my mind spinning. I didn't want to start taking medications. But I knew Dr. Shein was eager to help me. I knew she wouldn't do anything to harm me.

If the meds would help, I'd be crazy not to try them.

"I think you will see an improvement in less than a week," she said. She pulled a prescription pad from her desk drawer. She leaned over it and started to write the prescription.

After a few seconds, she looked up at me. "If you keep

seeing this creature, Lisa, I know a place to send you where there are experts at dealing with this kind of thing."

I jumped to my feet. "You mean a *mental hospital*?"

She nodded. "Well . . . yes. Let's not even think about that now, dear. Let's just get better—okay?"

43.

knew I shouldn't be sitting all alone in my room. I knew I'd start to brood and start to imagine things, and think about the nightmare my life had been for the past few months.

I stared at the boxes of pills on my dresser. I knew they would probably calm my brain and make me feel normal again. End my frightening fantasies. But I hadn't opened them yet. I kept staring at them and thinking about them. Once or twice, I opened a box and lifted the bottle out. But then I put it back down again.

And then suddenly, there I was sitting hunched on the edge of my bed—as if perched on the edge of the world. Any moment I felt I could fall off and plummet down . . . down . . . into the swirling fantasy world Dr. Shein said I was creating.

I shut my eyes and pictured Nate. Nate had been so sweet, so nice to me, so considerate and kind. I knew he didn't believe in my creature. But that didn't stop him from caring about me. He was there for me.

He was . . . well . . .

My thoughts changed. My brain slipped into a different gear as Nate's face lingered in my mind. And before I even realized, I was flooded by dark thoughts about him. Frightening thoughts about Nate that *couldn't* be true.

No way. No way.

I fought my own mind.

But I couldn't push the dark thoughts away.

And there was Summer, with her beautiful coppery hair, her high cheekbones, as pretty as a model, so willowy and graceful. Summer wanted to talk to me. She wanted to warn me—about Nate.

She said I didn't know what I was getting into. That I didn't have a clue about Nate.

When I told him about Summer's warnings, he laughed and said she was jealous.

And then Summer was dead. Brutally murdered outside Brenda Hart's house.

Nate had been there in the house that night. He was in the kitchen, and then he disappeared without telling me he was leaving. And after he vanished, the creature appeared.

Is it possible that Nate transforms into some kind of demon?

Is that what Summer wanted to warn me about?

Stop, Lisa. Stop these thoughts. They truly are insane. You really are crazy if you suspect Nate.

But what about Isaac?

Isaac kissed me and Nate saw it. Then Isaac was the next victim.

Summer, then Isaac. Nate had reason to be angry at them both. Reason to kill?

No way.

Stop it, Lisa.

I knew I should get up. Go out. Go do something. Stop these crazy thoughts. But I sat there hunched on the edge of my bed, hands flat on the mattress, staring down at the dark carpet, and thinking. . . .

And again I pictured the scratches down Nate's face. Long scratches down both cheeks. Could walking into a rosebush really make scratches like that?

He had to be lying, I decided.

He got those scratches while murdering Summer.

Suddenly, I felt certain that I had solved this horrifying mystery. Certain that I wasn't crazy. Certain that Nate was the demon, the demon of Fear Street.

I hugged myself as my whole body shuddered. Outside, clouds moved over the sun, and my room darkened as if my thoughts had darkened the world. The breeze through the window grew chilly. I stood up, walked to the window, glanced out at the cold, gray world out there, then shoved the window shut.

What could I do with my theory about Nate? Who could I tell?

If Nate found out that I knew the truth, I would definitely be his next victim.

Again, I pictured Summer, her copper hair spread over the ground, her head tilted at an impossible angle, her stomach ripped open, her glistening pink insides pouring out, puddling up on the grass.

I shuddered again and my phone rang.

I squinted at the screen. Nate.

I didn't want to answer, but my finger swiped the screen before I could stop myself. "Hello?"

"Lisa, hi. How's it going?"

"Okay, I guess."

"Listen, you and I have to talk. Can I come over now?"

44.

No . . . I . . . uh . . . I-I can't," I stuttered. I tried to force my voice to stay steady. I didn't want him to hear that I was suddenly frightened of him. "I have to go out with my mother," I lied.

"Maybe later?" Nate said. "I really need to tell you—"

"Yeah. Maybe later. I'll text you or something."

I clicked off. I was squeezing the phone so hard, my hand ached.

"I have to get out of here," I said to myself.

The phone rang again. Brenda Hart. Was she calling to fire me?

I hoped so. I didn't want to go back there. Who would want to go back to that place of horror and death?

Mom's arm was just about healed. The cast was coming off next week, so she could go back to work. I'd miss the money from the job, but it wasn't worth it.

I swiped my finger over the screen. "Hello? Brenda?"

"Lisa, please listen to me," she said, her voice tight,

urgent. "I know you probably don't want to come here again. I totally understand. But . . ." She hesitated.

She's not firing me?

"I have an emergency on my hands, Lisa. I've been called to a company meeting in Pittsburgh. It's kind of important. I need someone to stay with Harry overnight. Can you do it? Please—say you can do it."

The clouds lowered outside the window. The room grew even darker, as if a heavy blanket was settling over me. I realized I was gasping for breath.

I can't do this. This is suffocating me.

"I'll pay you double, Lisa," Brenda pleaded. "My sister can't take Harry. I need you to stay with him tonight. He misses you. He doesn't know anything about . . . about the dreadful things that have happened."

"Well . . ." The room was spinning. I stared into the deep gray outside the window. The world was suddenly black-and-white, as if I'd stepped into an old horror movie.

"Can you come, Lisa? Can you stay overnight with him?" Brenda asked.

I heard Harry shouting in the background. "Tell her to come. Tell her to come."

"Okay," I said. I said the word before I'd really decided. "Okay. What time do you want me?"

"Oh, thank you. I'm so grateful. Please come around six. Harry promises he'll go to bed early."

Harry *did* go to bed early. I had him tucked in at seven forty-five. He seemed tired the whole evening. He did a lot of loud yawning, and he barely touched the pasta Brenda had made for dinner.

After dinner, he cuddled up in my lap, and I read him some chapters from a sci-fi kids book about clones. He pressed his head against my shoulder and listened to every word. He smelled so sweet. I think he really wanted to be held. Maybe he was nervous because his mother was going away for the night.

Nate texted me at seven thirty. *Where r u? Wanna talk?*

I didn't reply. Just seeing his text made me shiver.

Of course, I made sure the doors were locked. And I shut all the windows even though it had turned into a steamy warm night.

After I tucked Harry in, I returned to the living room and walked over to the bookshelf where Brenda's photo albums were stacked. I wondered if there were photos of Nate and Saralynn in any of the albums I hadn't looked at.

I had a feeling . . . just a mild hunch . . . that maybe one of the albums would hold a clue for me. A clue to the truth about Nate. I was desperate for the tiniest bit of proof. Anything . . . anything at all that I could take to Captain Rivera and say, "Look at this. I'm not crazy."

I tugged out the second album on the pile, one I hadn't looked at on Friday night. I carried it to the couch and spread it open on my lap.

Again, there were photos of Brenda and the guy I

imagined was her husband. I flipped through quickly, searching for Nate and Saralynn. These photos were a little older than the ones in the first album. Harry appeared to be six or seven.

I was halfway through the album when my eyes settled on a photo of a teenage girl holding Harry on her lap. The photo was taken in this living room. The girl was sitting on this same couch.

Harry looked a little bit younger, but not much. He had one arm around the shoulder of the girl's pale blue sweater and one hand gripping a book they were reading.

I gazed at the photo. It caught my interest because the girl had such a sad expression on her face. Harry was grinning, his eyes wide. But the girl's face was drawn, her mouth pulled down, eyes blank, lifeless. She had stringy brown hair down the sides of her narrow face. One sleeve of her sweater was torn at the elbow.

Under the photo, someone had written the word *Joy* with a black marker.

Is that the girl's name? I wondered. *Or is it supposed to be a description of the scene?*

She didn't look joyful to me. As I stared, raising the album close to my face, I couldn't decide if she was sad or frightened.

As I started to return the album to my lap, a folded-up sheet of paper fell out. I closed the album and set it down on the couch cushion beside me. Then I picked up the paper and unfolded it.

It was a letter to Brenda. A very short letter, handwritten in small letters in dark blue ink. My eyes scanned down to the bottom. The letter was signed: *Sincerely, Joy.*

So, Joy *was* the girl's name.

Gripping the letter in both hands, I began to read.

32 Jamison Way
Shadyside

Dear Brenda:
I know you will understand why I can't babysit for
Harry anymore. He's a terrific boy. Really awesome.
And I loved taking care of him.

But so many frightening things. They . . . well, it
has all given me nightmares. Bad nightmares. I know it's
not your fault, but I can't sleep and I can't eat, and my
schoolwork is really in the pits.

My family really needs the money, but my mom says
I have to quit. And I think she's right.

I'm sorry. I know you have to go to work every
afternoon, and you need somebody. But it just can't
be me.

Please tell Harry I said bye.

Sincerely,
Joy

I read the letter through quickly. Then I went back to the top and read it slowly. By the time I finished the second reading, my hands were trembling. I tucked the letter back in the album.

It took awhile for the words to settle in my brain. It took me awhile to see clearly what the letter meant.

For one thing, Brenda had lied to me. When she interviewed me for the job, she said she was starting a new job and that's why she needed someone to stay with Harry. She said Harry had never had a babysitter.

But the letter and the photo proved that Joy had been the babysitter before me.

And Joy had to quit because frightening things were giving her nightmares.

Joy looked so sad and bedraggled, even with a grinning Harry on her lap. What had frightened her? What had given her the nightmares?

There was no clue in her letter. And no clue in the photo of her in the album.

I jumped to my feet. I felt a surge of excitement sweep down my body. I guess it was because I knew what I had to do.

I had to go see Joy. I had to talk to her as soon as I could.

45.

It took me a few days to find the time. I took the car. I told Mom I was going to the mall just to walk around and window-shop.

But I headed toward the address on Joy's letter. I knew where Jamison Way was. It was off the River Road in North Hills.

It was a bright afternoon, the sun golden and low in the sky. Right in my eyes as I followed the road along the Conononka River. Squinting into the glare on the windshield, I wished I'd remembered my sunglasses.

I kept picturing Joy, her name all wrong. Someone so sad-looking shouldn't be called Joy. I wanted her to tell me everything. I wanted to share my terrifying experiences in the house on Fear Street with her.

Would she talk with me? Would she want to talk about it with a total stranger?

I followed the River Road toward Jamison. Some

people were kayaking on the river, their yellow kayaks bobbing in the shimmering water.

Some people are having fun, I thought.

Yes, I was feeling sorry for myself. I barely had time to grieve for my father before the horrible murders began. Now everyone thought I was crazy, even my doctor.

Joy had to help me. She *had* to.

I turned onto Jamison and found myself driving past blocks of small redbrick houses set behind square lawns. Four or five kids were gathered around a wide-trunked tree at a corner house, shouting and gesturing. I realized they were trying to talk a cat down from a low limb.

I found 32 Jamison on the third block. The house had once been painted white but now the paint was peeling, and patches of redbrick showed through. An awning over the front window was torn and flapping in the warm breeze.

There were no driveways or garages with these houses. I parked Mom's car at the curb. Then I straightened my hair using the rearview mirror and climbed out of the car.

I could hear the kids cheering on the next block. I guessed they had succeeded in rescuing the cat.

Gazing at the concrete stoop in front of the small house, I began walking up the front lawn. I could tell it hadn't been mowed yet this spring. The ground beneath the sprawling grass was lumpy and hard.

A black mailbox was hung beside the front door. It had the number 32 in stenciled silver letters on the front. My chest felt fluttery as I climbed the two steps onto the stoop. I pressed the doorbell and took a deep breath.

Joy, please be home.

I didn't have to wait long. A short woman with cropped gray hair pulled the door open as if she'd been waiting in front of it. Her silver-gray eyes looked me up and down. Her face was overly made-up with bright red circles on her cheeks and thick lipstick over her mouth. She wore a black-and-yellow Steelers sweatshirt over gray sweatpants.

"Hello, I—"

"Can I help you?" she asked in a hoarse smoker's voice. Her face was tight with suspicion. She sneered. "You're too old to be selling Girl Scout Cookies."

That made her start to laugh, a dry raspy laugh that ended in a coughing fit.

"I . . . I'm looking for Joy," I said when she finally stopped hacking and coughing.

She winced. Her eyes bulged for a quick second. She narrowed the strange silvery eyes at me. "Is this a joke?"

"N-no," I stammered. "Does she live here? Is she your daughter? I really need to talk to her."

The woman sneered again, revealing yellowed teeth. "Did someone dare you to do this?" she demanded. "Did someone play a mean joke on you? Is that what this is?"

I swallowed. I took a step back and nearly toppled off the stoop. "No—" I started.

"Everyone knows Joy isn't here," the woman rasped.

"Do you know where she is?" I asked.

"Of *course* I know where my own daughter is," the woman snapped. "She's in the hospital, isn't she! She's in the hospital up in Martinsville. Why would you come looking for her here when she's in the state hospital?"

"I-I didn't know," I stammered. I backed off the stoop. "Really. I didn't know."

"Joy is in the state mental hospital!" the woman shouted. "She doesn't need any Girl Scout Cookies."

46.

I found the hospital after driving around the same neigh-
borhood twice. The streets in Martinsville are all one-
way and confusing, and even though it's the next town to
Shadyside, everyone always has to circle in on where they
are going. There's never a direct route to anywhere.

While I was driving, I had plenty of time to think. My
thoughts weren't bright or happy or hopeful. The more I
thought about Joy, the more I was frightened for myself.

She had the same job before me. She babysat for Brenda
Hart and took care of Harry. And terrible things happened.
Things frightening enough, horrifying enough to put her
in the state mental hospital.

Of course my biggest question was: *Am I next?*

The hospital was a tall, white stucco building with tall
hedges all around. Three cherry trees in the front had lost
most of their blossoms. I parked the car in a visitor parking lot and followed a narrow stone path to a side entrance.

A bronze plaque beside the door proclaimed that the

hospital was built by someone named Jacobus Fear in 1911. The silhouette of a face of a distinguished-looking man wearing a bowler hat was carved into the plaque.

At least they didn't call it Fear Hospital, I thought.

I was met at the door by a middle-aged man with shaggy white hair. He wore a gray uniform, like a custodian's uniform. His cheeks were bright pink and his blue eyes gleamed, as if he was happy to see me. His cheeks were so close-shaved, it looked like he had peeled off layers of his skin.

"I'd like to see one of the patients," I said.

He didn't reply. He held the door open, then led the way down a long dimly lit hallway of dark green walls and a hard tiled floor. The air smelled like cleaning products, very piney and sharp. I heard voices all down the hall, laughter and shouts, and music playing, some mellow rock tune I didn't recognize.

The man walked jauntily with his back straight up, shoulders back. He led me to a round desk in what had to be the front hall. A sign on the desk read: INFORMATION. But no one sat there.

The man smiled at me, his cheeks burning, and motioned for me to wait. Then he took my hand, raised it to his mouth, and *licked* it.

"Hey—!" Before I could pull my hand free, he slobbered all over the back of my hand. Then he uttered a short, high-pitched giggle. He turned and strode away, a strange stiff walk with his back as straight as an ironing board.

Well, what did I expect? I AM in a mental hospital.

I heard moans, sad moans, from a hallway on the other side of the desk. Someone shouted, "My cracker is on fire! My cracker is burning!"

Then silence.

A Barry Manilow song played from somewhere behind me.

I had a sudden strong feeling that I shouldn't be here. *I should have called ahead. What made me think it's okay to visit?*

Sure, I desperately wanted to talk to Joy. But the clatter of voices down the long halls, the sad cries and moans . . . the voices became noise. The noise turned into a roar.

I must have turned away from the desk because a woman appeared in the chair as if by magic. She had wavy brown hair tied back with a red hair scrunchy. She appeared to be fifty or so. She had a colorful scarf at the neck of her blouse and wore a dark business suit with a gold pin of a bird on one lapel.

She scrolled down the monitor in front of her and typed something, eyes reflecting the screen. Finally, she turned to me. "Sorry. I was on my break."

"No problem," I said. "I wasn't waiting long. I—"

"Did Travis lick your hand?" she asked.

I held it up for some reason. "Yes, he did."

She shook her head. Her eyes flashed with amusement. "He's a nice man. That's his way of showing that he likes you."

"I-I came to visit someone," I stammered. "Is it okay? I mean, are there visiting hours?"

Her expression turned serious. She glanced at her screen, then back at me. "Which patient would you like to see?"

I suddenly realized I didn't know her full name. "Uh . . . her name is Joy," I said.

She blinked. "Joy Fergus?"

I nodded.

The woman toyed with the bird pin on her lapel. "Are you a family member?"

"No. I'm a close friend," I lied.

"Well . . . I can check for you," she said, chewing her bottom lip. "But I'm afraid Joy isn't having one of her good days."

"Sorry," I murmured. "If I could only . . ."

She picked up the desk phone and talked to someone. Her eyes studied me while she talked. She tsk-tsked and talked some more in hushed tones I couldn't hear. "And what is your name?" she asked me, hanging up the phone.

I told her. She handed me a clipboard with some kind of form on it. "Just sign at the bottom," she said. "They will bring Joy to the library. You can talk to her there."

I signed it. My hand was shaking so hard I couldn't read my own name. I heard a howl from down the hall. And then someone giggling loudly. The two sounds blended together and rang off the walls of the waiting room.

The woman pointed down the hall to her right. "You'll

see the library. It's near the end of the hall." I thanked her. "Joy may seem different to you," she added. "She is slightly sedated, which makes her talk slowly. But she's doing very well. Most days."

I thanked her again. And stepped into the hallway. A cold feeling of dread swept over me as my shoes clicked over the hard floor. Doors on both sides of the hall were closed, but I could hear voices in almost every room.

A white-uniformed nurse with a tall Afro hairdo led a young woman past me. The woman was sobbing, dabbing at her face with a yellow handkerchief and sobbing so hard she struggled to breathe.

Joy Fergus was waiting for me in the library. I stopped at the doorway and studied her. The room looked like a comfortable living room with armchairs and couches and bookshelves against three walls. Pale light trickled in through a tall window in the back. Even though it was spring, a low fire burned in a brick fireplace.

I took a deep breath and stepped inside. Joy was sitting stiffly in a dark leather armchair. She turned as I entered.

She looked better than in the photograph I'd seen in Brenda's house. Her brown hair was pulled neatly back in a tight ponytail. She had pale orange lipstick on her lips, and her eyes were big and clear. She wore a long-sleeved blue tank top and baggy faded jeans with a hole on one knee.

"Hi," I said. I gave an awkward wave as I came close. "I'm Lisa."

She had a half-smile on her face, but it faded as I stepped

up to her chair. "They told me a friend came to see me. Are you my friend?"

I shook my head. "Sorry. I kinda lied about that."

She nodded. "Okay." Her voice was deep and smooth, velvety. I gazed at her. She seemed totally normal in every way. The only thing that marked her as a patient was the white name-bracelet around her left wrist.

"Can I sit down?" I asked, motioning to the armchair across from her.

"Sure," she said. She crinkled her forehead. "Do I know you?"

"No. I'll explain," I said. The armchair was softer than I expected and it made a loud *whoosh* as I sank into it.

"I h-have a problem with strangers," she stammered, lowering her dark eyes.

"I'm sorry," I said. "I won't keep you long. I just want to talk to you about—"

"Who are you?" she interrupted, eyeing me suspiciously. She tugged at the ID bracelet on her wrist. "Tell me. Who are you? Did they send you from school?"

"No," I said. "I'm sorry." She had been calm but now I could see she was getting agitated. She tugged at the bracelet, then clasped and unclasped her hands.

"Really. I'm sorry to bother you," I said. "You see . . . I babysit for Harry. Brenda Hart's son and—"

Her whole body arched up and went stiff. Her dark eyes bulged. She jumped to her feet. "I . . . can't talk about that."

"No. Just one minute. Please," I begged. I jumped up, too, and stood facing her. "I need to know—"

"I have nightmares," she said. Her smooth voice had become strained, harsh. "I have nightmares. That's why I have to stay here."

"I have nightmares, too," I said. "And I've seen things in the house. I've seen—"

She raised both hands and backed away from me. "I can't talk. Please go away."

"I just need to know some things," I insisted.

But she covered her ears with her hands. "I can't talk," she said through gritted teeth. "I can't talk. He's a demon. He's a monster."

I gasped. "You know Nate? Nate Goodman? Do you?"

"He's a demon!" she cried. "He's my nightmare. He's a demon!"

A stab of cold at the back of my neck froze me in place. "Nate—?" I gasped.

Joy stood red-faced, her hands still pressed tightly over her ears.

"Please, Joy," I begged. "Tell me—"

"He's a demon."

The door swung open, and two nurses burst in, eyes on Joy. They grabbed her arms gently. One of them smoothed a hand down her back, petting her, comforting her. The other one turned to me: "Don't blame yourself. She has these bad days. It's not your fault."

47.

Nate wasn't in school. Someone said he had a virus or something. Saralynn said she hadn't talked to him. She had been away doing college visits with her parents in Boston.

Saralynn wants to study to be a nutritionist. Sure, she hangs out at Lefty's like the rest of us, gobbling his two-dollar double cheeseburgers. But she thinks she can improve people's lives by teaching them the right way to eat. She says she will probably become a vegan some day. But not till after high school because Lefty's hamburgers are so good.

I cornered her in the hall before third-period study hall to question her about Nate. "Why was Summer coming to warn me about him?" I demanded.

Saralynn leaned back against a locker. "Beats me. They went out together for a while in tenth grade. I think maybe she was too intense for him or something."

"Did she know something bad about Nate?" I asked.

Saralynn scrunched up her face. "Bad about Nate? Like what?"

I shrugged. "You're his cousin. Is there something weird about Nate?"

"Lisa, you mean because of his horror collection?"

"No," I said. "Something weirder."

"Nate is Nate," she replied. "What do you want me to say?"

I want you to tell me if he turns into a demon late at night and murders and eats people he doesn't like. I want you to tell me if he terrified Harry's last babysitter and drove her crazy.

I want you to tell me if I'm in danger.

The bell rang. The hall emptied out as everyone headed to class.

"I can't tell you anything," Saralynn said. "Sorry." She turned and headed down the hall, her backpack bouncing on her back.

I picked up Harry at Alice's house at four. Harry grabbed my hand. He was eager to go home. He wore a funny SpongeBob T-shirt and baggy white shorts that seemed way too big for him. He had a smear of chocolate on his chin.

"Alice said we can bake brownies when we get home," he said, tugging my hand hard. His blue eyes pleaded with me. "Can we?"

"Well . . ."

"Brenda left a box of brownie mix for you on the sink,"

Alice said, appearing behind me. She had a stack of folded laundry in her arms.

"Nice," I said.

Alice narrowed her eyes at Harry. "You can have brownies tonight if you promise to go to bed on time."

Harry raised his right hand and uttered in a deep voice, "I swear."

For some reason, that made Alice and me both laugh. I guess it was the solemn way Harry said it.

"Okay, brownie night tonight," I said. Harry tugged me to the back door. I called goodbye to Alice and followed him outside.

A sunny afternoon, warm with a cool breeze shaking the fresh spring leaves so that the trees all seemed to be whispering. Two robins were ducking their beaks into the back lawn, pulling up fat brown earthworms.

Harry and I strolled to the front of the house, then along the sidewalk toward his house. Joy was on my mind. I hadn't stopped thinking about her. I decided I had to ask Harry about her.

"Did you have a babysitter before me?" I asked.

He nodded. "Yes."

"What was her name?"

"Joy. She was nice, but she had to leave."

"Why did she have to leave?" I asked him.

The sun washed over his blond hair and made it glow. His blue eyes stared up at me. He didn't answer.

"Why did Joy leave?" I repeated.

"Mom said she got sick." He kicked a small stone to the curb. He ran ahead and kicked it again. The conversation had ended.

Joy got sick all right, I thought. *Something happened that sent her to a mental hospital.*

We'd walked a full block. I suddenly realized Harry was traveling a little light. "Harry—your backpack?"

His eyes went wide. "Uh-oh. I left it at Alice's." He raised his hands in a begging pose. "Can we leave it there?"

"And not do your homework tonight?"

He nodded with a grin.

"No way." I stopped him with both hands on his shoulders. "You stay right here. Don't move. I'll get it."

I turned and took off running before he could argue. My shoes thudded the grass as I darted through the front lawns of the houses I'd passed. A few seconds later, I stepped into Alice's kitchen, breathing hard.

No sign of her in the kitchen. "Alice? It's only me," I called.

I hurried to the little office at the side of the house where Harry and Alice held their classes together. Harry's backpack was usually on the table they used, but not today. I didn't see it in the living room, either.

Did he leave it in the kitchen?

I was halfway through the back hall when I heard the howls.

I stopped. And listened. The cries sounded so sad. And so human.

Definitely not a cat.

Such sad, desperate howls for help. From the basement?

I hesitated at the top of the basement stairs. Then I grabbed the wooden banister and made my way down the stairs.

I was nearly to the bottom when I turned and saw who was howling.

And then my startled scream echoed through the basement.

48.

"N*oooo*. Oh, no," I moaned. "No. Please. It can't be."

Still on the steps, I stared at the three cages lined up against the basement wall. Three cages with three creatures, one in each cage.

They were hunched low because the cages weren't tall enough for them to stand. They gripped the bars with long bonelike fingers. And howled in almost-human voices, so high and shrill and filled with pain.

"*Ellpusssss,*" the nearest to me hissed.

I couldn't breathe. I couldn't move off the steps. They were so sad and ugly. Human monsters. Like the demon I saw in Brenda Hart's house. Only their faces were more twisted and wrong and hideous.

One of them had an empty eye socket where one eye should be. The creature in the next cage had tiny arms, too short . . . too short for his body. The third creature . . . his bottom jaw was missing. No lips, only long upper teeth that hung straight down and a fat tongue that seemed to spring from deep in his throat.

Half of his face is missing.

I felt my stomach lurch. A wave of nausea swept over me. I started to vomit. Choking, gagging, I somehow forced it down.

On shaky legs, I left the stairway behind and stepped closer to the cages. I couldn't believe my eyes. The creatures were so hideous, so malformed, and so sad. Their bodies were bent. Their arms were too short and too skinny. Their faces had pieces missing.

They howled and wailed and thumped the bars with their small fists as they saw me approach.

This is not an hallucination.

These creatures are real.

What are they doing down here?

I screamed again. I couldn't hold it back.

And one of the creatures reached through the bars, wrapped his hot, dry fingers around my wrist—and pulled me to him.

"No. Please—let go! Let *go* of me!" I gasped.

49.

The fingers tightened around my wrist. I cried out in pain and terror and tried to pull back. But the creature's skin was rough as sandpaper, and as pain shot down my arm, I thought the creature had cut through my wrist.

All three of them were howling now, hopping up and down like gorillas, drooling and snapping their jaws.

With a sharp twist, I tried to squirm from the creature's grasp. But he pulled me against the cage. Grunting, he slid his twisted face to the bars—and *spat* on my cheek.

"Ohhhhhhhh." A moan of horror escaped my throat. His tongue was sandpaper scratchy too, and left a prickly trail of hot saliva on my cheek. My whole body shuddered.

As the other two demons shrieked and howled, I turned and stared into the cage. This one had no bottom jaw. But he pushed his face against the bars, trying to scrape my face with his upper teeth.

"Let go!" I screamed. But my voice was drowned out

by their howls and screeches. I wanted to cover my ears. The horrible cries sent chill after chill down my back.

"Let goooo!"

The creature spit at me again. This time the big gob of saliva flew over my head.

I ducked—and to my surprise—tugged my hand free. "Hey—!" With a startled cry, I stumbled away from the cage. I couldn't catch my balance. I slammed hard into the basement wall. Pain shot down my shoulder.

I didn't care. I was free.

I rubbed my wrist. The creature's fingers had squeezed a red band around my wrist. I took one last look at the three of them, still hopping up and down, hooting and grunting, their deep, sad eyes on me. Then, gasping for breath, I turned and stumbled up the basement steps.

At least now I have proof.

I'm not crazy. The creatures exist. I didn't imagine the one in Brenda's house.

I have proof. Got to call the police.

I climbed to the hallway and slammed the basement door shut. Still no sign of Alice. She must have gone out.

Alice lied to me that first day. She said I heard her cat down there. Why did she have three monsters caged in her basement?

I knew I couldn't think about that now. Let the police sort it out.

I found Harry's backpack on the floor, leaning against the kitchen counter. I grabbed it up and, with the animal howls and cries repeating in my ears, I pulled open the kitchen door and flung myself outside.

Harry was waiting obediently where I left him. "Where were you?" he demanded. "What took you so long?"

I handed him his backpack. Then I mopped sweat off my forehead with the back of my hand. "I . . . uh . . . couldn't find it," I said.

He squinted at me, shielding his eyes from the lowering afternoon sun. "Why is your hair all messed up?"

"Wind blew it, I guess." I tried to straighten it with my hands.

"I'm starving," he said. "Can we have dinner right away?"

"Sure. No problem." We started to walk. He didn't strap on his backpack. He swung it in front of him in both hands.

"Did you ever go down in your aunt's basement?" I asked, trying to make the question sound unimportant.

He shook his head. "No. Why?"

"Just wondered."

"Aunt Alice said it's messy and I shouldn't go down there."

We crossed the street. A blue SUV rumbled past. Someone waved to me from the driver's seat but I couldn't see who it was.

"Does Alice have a cat?" I asked him.

He nodded. "Mister Puffball."

"I haven't seen Mister Puffball," I said. "What does he look like?"

Harry shrugged. "He never comes out. He's very shy."

"Does he stay in the basement?"

Harry didn't answer. He took off, running up the front lawn to his house, swinging the backpack in front of him.

He's at Alice's house all the time, I thought. *How come he has never heard the creatures in the basement? How does Alice keep them quiet?*

Again, I figured the police could find the answer to all my questions. Rubbing my throbbing wrist, I knew I'd never forget the horrors of that basement. But at the same time I felt relieved, relieved that I wasn't an insane person seeing horror-movie creatures that didn't exist.

I couldn't wait to call the police. I made Harry his dinner, microwave pizza and a small salad. Then I left him in the kitchen to eat and made my way to the den where I could call without him hearing.

I pulled Captain Rivera's card from my wallet. My hand trembled as I punched in the number.

Finally. Finally, he has to believe me.

I was passed along to two other officers until I was connected to the captain. "Rivera," he answered in a grunt.

"I'm not crazy," I blurted out. "I've seen other creatures. I've seen them. I'm not crazy."

50.

A long silence at the other end. Then Rivera finally spoke up. "Who is this?"

"Oh. Sorry." I shut my eyes. I felt like an idiot. "It's Lisa. Lisa Brooks."

"Oh. Yes? What do you want?"

"I'm not crazy. I've been telling the truth," I said. "The demons are real."

Another silence. Then: "Lisa, have you seen your doctor?"

"No. Listen to me. Captain Rivera, this time you have to listen. I saw three other creatures. In cages."

"Three horror-movie creatures in cages?"

"Yes. One of them grabbed me. They were screaming and howling and jumping up and down, and he grabbed me by the wrist and—"

"I'm sorry. You're not helping me, Lisa. I have a murder investigation to run here, and it isn't going well."

"I *am* helping you," I insisted.

"I'm sorry about your accident," he said. "Sorry you're having problems. But—"

"Just give me one more chance," I begged. "Just believe me this one time. Just this once. And if it turns out I'm crazy . . . I'll never bother you again. I swear."

"I really can't—"

"Just come to Harry's aunt's house and look in the basement. It won't take any time at all. You'll see that I'm not crazy. You'll see that I'm not making this up. These creatures are real and . . . and . . ."

I had to take a breath. The words poured out of me like a rushing waterfall. I knew I sounded like a crazy nut. But I was so desperate to make him believe me, to show him what I found.

"Just this once!" I screamed. "You'll thank me. I *swear* you'll thank me."

"Okay," he said abruptly. "Okay, okay. Stop shouting in my ear."

I swallowed. "You'll come?"

"Give me the address. I'll be right there. I was taking a supper break anyway."

"Oh. Okay. Great." It took me a few seconds to realize I had won.

I gave him the address. "I'll meet you over there," I said. "They're in the basement. You'll see."

I clicked off. I heard Harry calling me from the kitchen. Harry. I'd almost forgotten about him. What could I do with him while I ran back to Alice's house? I couldn't take him there. And, of course, I wasn't supposed to leave him on his own.

But I had no choice.

I trotted back into the kitchen. "Do you want more food?"

He burped really loudly. Then he rubbed his stomach. "No, I'm full. Do I have to do my homework now?"

"Would you like to play your Xbox game?" I asked.

"Yes. Yes! Can I?"

"I have to run out for two minutes," I said. "If you promise you'll sit in the living room and play your game, and *not move or do anything else,* I'll let you play it now."

He squinted at me. "You're going out?"

I nodded. "Just for two minutes. Maybe five. I swear. Will you do it? Will you sit still and play your game?"

He pumped his fists in the air. "Yes! Sweet!"

"And don't tell your mom I ran out for a few minutes?" I said.

He grinned. "If you let me stay up late."

I narrowed my eyes at him. "Excuse me?"

"I won't tell her if you promise you'll let me stay up late."

I sighed. "Harry, you know it isn't good for you."

"Promise?" he insisted. "Promise?"

I had to get over to Alice's. I didn't have time to argue with him. "Okay," I said. "You can stay up late. I promise."

I got him set up. I made sure the doors were locked. Then

I hurried out the front door, down the lawn, onto Fear Street.

The late afternoon sun was a red ball, ducking behind the trees, sending long shadows across the lawn. The air had grown cooler. It smelled flowery and sweet. The people on the corner had mowed their lawn, and the aroma of cut grass greeted me as I crossed the street.

I cut through backyards and then a narrow gravel alley. I came to the corner of Alice's block just as Rivera's patrol car pulled to the curb. Rivera climbed out. I waved to him as I ran.

His black uniform shirt was rumpled. His eyes were hidden behind dark glasses. I could hear the rattle of the police radio as he slammed the car door.

"You didn't have to come, Lisa." His eyes were on the house.

"But I wanted to be there when you found them," I said. "I mean, it's important to me, too. I know you think I'm crazy and—"

He waved me quiet with one hand. "I don't think you're crazy. Let's not talk about that now. Let's just have a look in the basement. Then we can decide who's crazy."

I think maybe he was making a joke, but I wasn't sure. His face was like dark-stained wood. Hard. His features didn't move.

I followed him up the driveway. Alice appeared in the door before we reached the stoop. She had pink plastic curlers in her hair. She squinted at me. "Lisa? Is something wrong? Is Harry okay?"

"He's fine," I answered. I suddenly felt embarrassed. I'd just turned Alice in to the police. Maybe I shouldn't have come with Rivera.

"Harry is fine," I said. "I just—"

Rivera stepped in front of me. "Good afternoon. I'm very sorry to trouble you. I had a report . . ."

"A report?" Alice's face twisted in confusion. "Why don't you come in." She held the door open and stepped aside.

I followed Captain Rivera into the living room. His gaze darted around the room. I couldn't decide what to do with my hands. I kept shoving them into my jeans pockets, then pulling them out.

"I hope this isn't too big an inconvenience," Rivera said softly. "I wonder if I could just take a quick glance at your basement."

Why was he being so polite to her? She was keeping ugly, deformed MONSTERS down there.

Alice put a hand to her throat. Her eyes widened in surprise. "My basement?"

She's a good actress, I thought. *She's acting totally innocent.*

"You want to see my basement?" she said. "Is there some kind of problem?"

"I hope not," Rivera answered, eyeing me.

I hung back by the living room doorway. I had my arms crossed tightly in front of me. My legs felt shaky, weak. I pointed to the back wall. "The basement stairs are over there," I told Rivera.

"I don't have a warrant or anything . . ." Rivera said to her.

"No worries." Alice led the way across the room. "I can't imagine why there might be a problem in my basement, Officer. You say you had a report?"

Rivera nodded. "Do I have your permission to look downstairs?"

Alice held open the door. "Go ahead. No problem at all." She clicked the basement light switch.

Rivera's shoes clumped heavily as he made his way down the narrow stairway. Alice started to block my way. I could see she wanted to ask me what was up.

But I slid past her into the stairwell and followed Rivera. I was two-thirds of the way down the stairs when I stopped and gazed around. I saw an old couch draped in a bed sheet, a stack of old magazines, a few random cartons against one wall.

Rivera, halfway across the basement floor, turned and narrowed his eyes at me. "Well?"

I spun away from him. I couldn't bear to face him. *Ohmigod. Ohmigod.*

The basement was empty. No cages. No creatures.

Then, from between two stacks of cartons, I saw a pair of eyes glaring out at me. "There!" I screamed to Rivera and pointed.

I gasped as a large gray-and-white cat stepped out. He

bent his back, stretched and yawned. His eyes glowed a pale green.

"Mister Puffball!" Alice cried. "I've been looking for you."

51.

Alice lifted the big cat and hugged it. "You've been a bad boy, hiding down here." She turned to Rivera. "Are we done here?"

He nodded. "Yes. Thank you. I appreciate your cooperation." He was staring at me. I knew what he was thinking: *You're crazy, Lisa.*

I hurried up the stairs first because I didn't want to confront Alice. How could I explain this to her? I knew she'd tell Brenda about it. I was definitely out of a job.

Outside, Rivera patted me on the shoulder, but his expression was cold. "I don't know what to say, Lisa," he said in a voice just above a whisper. "Are you seeing your doctor regularly?"

I nodded.

"I'm trying not to be harsh," he said, his eyes locked on mine. "But I have two murders to solve, and I can't have you wasting my time."

He didn't give me a chance to reply. He strode quickly

down the front lawn to his patrol car. He was shaking his head as he walked.

He thinks I'm a nutcase.

"But I'm not," I murmured to myself. Those sad creatures were real. I had the red bruise on my wrist to prove it.

Why didn't I show it to Captain Rivera? He probably wouldn't believe a creature did it to me. After this, I knew he wouldn't believe a word I said.

But I knew I wasn't crazy. And I knew those caged monsters were real.

Did Alice see me go down in the basement? Is that why she moved them somewhere so quickly?

And then another question rushed into my troubled thoughts: How does Nate fit in here? If he is Brenda's cousin, that means he is Alice's cousin, too. But what is the connect between Nate and those three deformed creatures?

I was convinced that Nate was behind the two gruesome murders. He had been texting me and calling and, so far, I'd been able to avoid him.

My head swam in confusion. I thought I cared about Nate. But now I realized I was terrified of him. I knew that his horror collection wasn't just a hobby. It was the *real him*.

As Rivera's car pulled away from the curb, I suddenly remembered Harry.

I promised him I'd be back in five minutes. But it had been more than fifteen.

Alice called to me from her front stoop, but I pretended I didn't hear her and took off running. A few minutes later, I burst through the kitchen door, calling to Harry. "Are you okay? Harry? Everything okay?"

I shouldn't have worried. He was still sitting in the glow of the screen, his eyes intent on his game. I dropped into the nearest chair, still breathing hard from running all the way back.

"Where did you go?" he asked, without taking his eyes from the screen.

"Just to Alice's," I said. "You know you're going to sprain both thumbs if you keep playing so long. You'll get thumb sprains and your thumbs will turn blue."

He laughed. "I don't think so."

"Well, it's getting late," I said, stepping between him and the screen. "I'm sorry to say it, but it's homework time."

He set down the controller. "Remember? You said I could stay up late?"

"I know," I said, patting his shoulder. "But it's a bad idea. If your mom finds out . . ."

"You PROMISED!" he cried. "You PROMISED." He sounded so hurt, hurt that I would break a promise.

"You're right," I said, backing down. "When you're right, you're right. You get to stay up late tonight."

That brought a big smile to his face. When he smiled like that, the most adorable dimples popped up on his cheeks. He hugged me around the waist.

"Stop! Too tight! Too tight!" I cried, prying his arms away.

He laughed. "I'm strong."

"How did you get so cute?" I asked him.

"Practice," he said.

His answer startled me so much, I burst out laughing. And then we were both laughing. It was such a perfectly silly answer.

We spread his math notebook on the kitchen table, and I helped him with the story problems. He didn't need much help. He's very smart and quick and has a good mind for math.

Math always made my brain hurt. I just don't have that orderly, logical kind of mind, I guess. I'm a good student. School is pretty easy for me. But I always have to work hard in math classes just to keep up with everyone else.

After the math, he had a story to read with questions to answer at the end. I sat across from him and watched him read. He had tremendous concentration. He never raised his eyes from the page until the story was finished.

His homework finished, I made a big bowl of microwave popcorn and we settled on the living room couch to watch a Disney cartoon on Netflix. He laughed and clapped his hands as he watched. He bounced up and down. He seemed to get more energy as the time grew later.

I couldn't concentrate on the movie. Every sound, every rattle or creak in the house made me jump. And my eyes kept wandering to the top of the stairs where I'd seen the green-faced demon last time.

I kept glancing at my phone. Did Nate plan to visit us again tonight?

"Stop bouncing up and down," I said, tugging Harry to the couch cushion beside me. "You're making me seasick."

He laughed. Then he took the controller and paused the movie. He turned to me, his eyes wide, an open-mouthed grin spread over his pale face.

"I like staying up late, Lisa."

"It's not a good idea," I said. "You're going to get me in trouble, Harry."

"I like staying up late," he repeated. His blue eyes suddenly had an unnatural glow. "Know why I like it so much?"

"Why?" I said.

"Because I get to change. It's so much fun."

I squinted at him, confused. "Change?" I said. "What do you mean change?"

"Watch," he said. He stood up. He turned and faced me. His grin faded. He made a soft grunting sound. Behind him, the TV was frozen in a cartoon scene with a dragon snorting fire.

Harry took a step back. His eyes rolled up in his head.

I gasped in alarm. "Harry—what are you doing?" I cried.

"Changing," he whispered. His hair seemed to sink into his head. Instantly. His hair disappeared except for a strip of black fur down the middle of his scalp.

His nose poked forward until it became a snout. His mouth twisted. Long jagged teeth made a *ripping* sound as they poked out of his gaping pink gums. His blue eyes appeared to burst into flame—and now they were a burning red, deep in their sockets.

"Harry—" I choked out. "It's you. It's you. You're the demon!"

He tossed back his head and let out a long, snakelike hiss. The hiss turned into dry laughter, laughter that sounded like someone vomiting, dry heaves of laughter, cold, evil laughter.

The chilling laughter of a monster.

52.

Nooooo!" A scream burst from my throat.

I tried to climb up from the couch, but he shoved me back down with startling strength. A dry rattle escaped his open snout, a snake's rattle. And he leaped on me, pinning me to the couch.

His ruby eyes rolled crazily in their sockets. His jaw snapped, the big teeth clicking. Beads of sweat formed on his green-tinted skin.

"Let me up! Let me out of here!" I shrieked.

But he had me pinned to the back of the couch. And then he raised his hands. I saw the long fingers. The long, skinny fingers. He dug them into my hair. He began pulling at my hair, rattling and hissing, the fingers sharp and hard, scraping my scalp.

"Let go! Get off!"

I tried to push the creature but he was too strong.

He snapped at me. I felt a sharp pain at my earlobe. He snapped again. Missed. Did he plan to *eat my ears*?

I squirmed and ducked as his jaws opened and closed, and his long tongue rubbed against my cheek, rubbed and pressed, scratched my face, the hot dry tongue, licking so hard as he rattled.

He's going to kill me. Like the others. Like the others. He's going to tear me apart and EAT my insides.

I tried to scream again but no sound came out. He held my head tightly between his snakelike fingers. Held me in place, pressing those ugly hands against my cheeks. As he held me down, he opened his snout and began to lower it.

He's going to eat my face!

His hot, sour breath burned my cheeks. The eyes shimmered and glowed, buried deep in their sockets. The jagged teeth were drenched in drool.

I shut my eyes. I held my breath. I gritted my teeth.

And waited for the crushing pain.

Waited.

No.

I heard a voice. "I don't believe it!" A woman's voice.

I opened my eyes to see Brenda. Harry still drooling and hissing on top of me. And Brenda, hands angrily on her waist, leaning over the back of the couch.

"Lisa!" she cried. "What have you *done*?"

53.

*H*ow *could* you?" Brenda screamed. "You let him stay up late."

She darted around the side of the couch. She grabbed Harry by the back with both hands—and tore him off me. She swung him to the floor and held him there.

The creature didn't resist. He didn't try to fight her. And slowly he transformed back to Harry. The black fur slid into his scalp and the curly blond hair shot up. He shut his eyes, and when he opened them, they were big and blue again. The green tint faded from his skin as the snout receded, and his face reappeared, his normal face, so innocent-looking now.

In fact, he looked a little embarrassed. He hunched his slender shoulders. He half-turned so we couldn't see his face.

I jumped to my feet, wiping thick saliva off my cheeks. I struggled to straighten my hair. My heart was pounding so hard, I felt my chest might explode.

Brenda stood facing me, her fists clenched at her sides,

her jaw clenched, her expression angry. "I warned you, Lisa," she said through gritted teeth. "I warned you."

"I—I didn't know—"

I stood there, frozen, still terrified. I didn't know what she expected me to say. Did she expect me to apologize for keeping her son up late? Her son who turns into a demon?

"I-I'm going," I stammered. I took a step toward the front.

She moved quickly to block my path. "I'm sorry. I can't let you go home, Lisa."

"But—" I tried to dodge around her, but she was too quick for me. She bumped me hard with her shoulder. I stumbled back, struggling to stay on my feet.

"You can't leave, Lisa," she said. "You've seen what Harry is. I can't let you tell anyone."

"But . . . but . . ." I sputtered. "I don't understand, Brenda," I said, finally finding my voice. "He's a killer. He's a monster. You can't let him—"

"I know he's been bad," she said. "But I can control him."

"*Control* him?" I cried. "He . . . he killed Summer and Isaac."

"I know," she said. "But that wasn't *his* fault—it was *yours.*"

"Mine?" I cried. "My fault? The two murders were my fault? Are you crazy?"

"You let him stay up late," she said, sneering. "You had instructions. Everyone would have been safe if you had followed them. But you let him stay up. Even after I warned you."

"You didn't warn me that he's a *demon!*" I screamed. I glanced around frantically, looking for an escape route.

The bowl of popcorn, half-empty, still stood on the coffee table. The TV was still frozen on the cartoon dragon. Normal life. They were signs of normal life.

But my normal life had ended.

Harry stood behind me, his hands in his jeans pockets, blond hair catching the light, a strange smile on his face. Brenda stayed close in front of me, readying herself in case I tried to run again.

"You can't keep me here," I said. "Brenda, you have to know that—"

She raised a hand to silence me. Her eyes were on Harry. "He's all I've got in the world," she whispered. "He's all I've got. I'm bringing him up . . . bringing him up for the others."

The others?

"Huh? What others?" I blurted out.

"You don't know anything—*do* you?" she cried.

"No. How *could* I?" I screamed.

I thought Nate was the demon. I had everything wrong.

"My family is bringing him up," Brenda said. "Nate and Saralynn and Alice and I have a big responsibility."

I gasped. "Nate and Saralynn know about it? They know Harry is a monster?"

"He's not a monster." Brenda scowled at me. Her voice

trembled with emotion. "The *first* three were monsters. They couldn't transform into humans. They were defective. Failures. Failures that must be kept hidden away. But Harry—Harry is perfect. We made him and we're bringing him up and . . ."

I didn't hear the rest of what she was saying. I could only think about Nate and Saralynn. I thought they were my friends. But they knew all along. They knew who murdered Summer and Isaac, and they kept it a secret.

They are all raising some kind of demon they created.

"I can't let you ruin everything, Lisa." Brenda's voice returned to my consciousness.

"Brenda, please—" I pleaded.

"I can't let you leave this house alive. The others are depending on me to bring Harry up to maturity."

Harry had been standing there silently, hands in his pockets, eyes on Brenda. But now, a wide grin spread across his cute face. And as he grinned, he began to change. Once again, his blond hair receded into his scalp and the strip of black fur replaced it. His snout grew long and his eyes flared red.

Grunting and wheezing, he became the demon again. He snapped his jaw and eyed me hungrily. Thick white drool ran down his chin.

"I can't let you. I can't let you."

I'd been staring in horror at Harry as he changed. I didn't realize Brenda had left the room. But I turned at the sound of her voice and saw her darting back from the kitchen.

I gasped when I saw the large kitchen knife in her hand, the long blade gleaming in the light from the ceiling.

I froze. The demon Harry stepped closer to keep me from escaping.

"I'm afraid you're going to have a very bad accident with this knife!" Brenda exclaimed.

"No. Please—" I uttered in a choked whisper.

Her eyes bulged as she leaped at me—and stabbed me in the chest.

54.

No. I moved before the blade came down.

I threw myself to the floor. And the knife stabbed the air above my head. I felt the whoosh of the blade over my hair.

She swung the knife again, and I rolled right into her. I bumped her shins hard and sent her tumbling to the floor. She landed on her back, and the knife sailed out of her hand and across the carpet.

She groaned and started to her feet. But I jumped on top of her and tried to pin her to the floor. We struggled and wrestled, rolling over the carpet.

Behind me, I glimpsed the demon Harry move toward the knife. His shoulders were heaving up and down, and he snapped his jaw excitedly.

I rolled off Brenda and made a wild dive for the knife.

Missed.

Harry grabbed it and wrapped his snakelike fingers around the handle.

He stood over me. I was helpless, on my knees on the floor. He raised the knife high in the air—

—and a loud crash made him turn.

I turned, too, and saw Nate bursting through the front window. He landed on both feet, his eyes on the demon Harry and the raised knife.

Nate uttered a furious scream as he came running into the room. He lifted a tall, blue lamp off the table beside the couch—and smashed it over Harry's head.

Harry groaned and sank to the floor. He folded up onto his stomach, the knife beneath him. He didn't move.

"What have you done?" Brenda shrieked. "Are you crazy? What have you done to Harry?"

Red-faced, waving her fists, she leaped at Nate. He wrapped his arms around her waist, pinning her arms at her sides, and held her helpless. She struggled to squirm free, but he was too strong for her. He twisted her around and sent her spinning onto the couch.

"Nate—what are you doing here?" I cried.

"I knew you were in trouble, Lisa," he said, watching Brenda warily. "I wanted to explain everything. I wanted to tell you why Saralynn pretended not to see the demon Friday night. I wanted to tell you how Saralynn and I are responsible for bringing him up, too. But . . . but . . ."

Brenda jumped to her feet.

Nate arched his back, tensed his fists, prepared for a fight.

"Run, Lisa," he urged, giving me a gentle push. "Run. Get out of here. Now!"

I hesitated for a second. But then I took off, running on trembling legs to the front door. I didn't look back. I heard Brenda's angry shrieks. I could hear them scuffle.

"Don't let her get away! She'll spoil everything!" Brenda cried.

"No. This has to stop, Brenda. I won't let you kill her. This has to stop!"

Then I was out the door, Nate's cries ringing in my ears. Out into the night, the cool air fresh against my burning face. I ran, ran down Fear Street. Deserted. No one outside. No cars. Nothing moving. The houses mostly dark.

I ran down Fear Street, not thinking, not seeing anything at all. Just ran for my life. And all the way down the street, I could hear the furious screams, Brenda's angry protests.

A block away, I could still hear her wailing and shrieking. Frightening sounds I knew would stay with me forever.

55.

The next morning, I paced back and forth across Dr. Shein's office. I was too tense and too upset to sit in the chair across from her desk. She kept her eyes on me as I walked, her face expressionless, her hands clasped in her lap.

The desk phone rang, but she ignored it. A fly buzzed around her head but she ignored that, too. I'd been talking for nearly ten minutes, but it was hard to keep the story straight.

"Go on," she said. "Don't worry about telling it in order. Just tell me what you saw and what happened last night."

My hands were ice cold. I rubbed them in front of me as I paced. "The police don't believe me," I said. "My own mother doesn't believe me. No one believes me. Everyone thinks I'm crazy."

"They think you're *troubled*," she interrupted. "You shouldn't say they think you're *crazy*."

"Whatever," I said. I stopped walking and faced her.

"Whatever. Whatever. That boy really is a demon, Dr. Shein. Brenda Hart is raising a demon in that house."

She opened a black-covered notebook and scribbled in it for a few seconds. My chest felt fluttery. I kept feeling cold, then hot. I'd never been as nervous.

I took a few steps toward her desk. Then I plopped into the chair. I couldn't walk anymore. My legs were too rubbery. I pulled out my iPhone and pressed it into my lap.

"And there are others," I said. "Other demons. Experiments that went wrong. Really."

She eyed me, then scribbled some more.

"I saw them in cages in Alice's basement," I said. "Only when I brought Captain Rivera there, they were gone. Alice had moved them."

Dr. Shein tapped the pencil eraser against the glass desktop. Behind her glasses, her eyes narrowed till they were nearly shut. I could see she was concentrating, thinking hard.

"This must be so frightening for you," she said finally. "I'm so sorry you are experiencing this, Lisa. And I'm glad I'm here. I know how alone you feel now. And I'm glad I'm here so you have someone to trust, someone you can confide in."

I swallowed. "Does that mean you believe me? Really?" I asked in a meek voice. "You are my last hope, Dr. Shein. Do you believe me?"

She hesitated. "Yes, I believe you," she said finally.

"Oh, thank goodness!" I cried. "Thank you. Thank you."

"I believe you," Dr. Shein repeated. "In fact, I *know* you're telling the truth."

"I'm so relieved," I said. "Thank you!"

She stood up. "I know you're telling the truth, Lisa. That's why I'm going to find you a nice hospital where you will be comfortable for a long time."

I gasped. My hands shot up to my cheeks. "Hospital? Huh? What do you mean?"

"A long, long hospital stay," she said in a voice just above a whisper. "We can't have you telling people about us, Lisa. It just wouldn't do."

56.

She pressed both hands on her desktop and leaned forward, her eyes locked on me. "You understand why you have to go away, don't you?"

She waited for me to answer, but I remained perfectly still, gripping my phone, my heart fluttering in my chest.

"You are seeing things, Lisa," she continued. "It doesn't matter if they are real or not. You are seeing things you shouldn't."

She forced a smile. It was an ugly, cold smile. "I'm going to order a nice long hospital stay for you, Lisa. A long hospital stay, maybe a year or two, with *other* patients who see things."

Like Joy, I thought. I pictured her—Harry's previous babysitter—locked away in that mental hospital in Martinsville. That hospital! I saw *myself* there, drugged, helpless, the crazy girl who sees monsters. . . .

A powerful chill rolled down my back.

"When you get out," Dr. Shein continued, "no one will ever believe you. No one. And we can all get on with our mission and with our lives."

"I-I don't understand," I stammered. "You picked me to babysit Harry. Why? Why me?"

She pulled the chair out and sat back down at her desk. She picked up the pencil and rolled it between her fingers as she watched me.

"I picked you because you were so traumatized," she said. "You had a severe concussion. You were having dark nightmares and hallucinations. You were a perfect choice."

"Perfect?"

"Of course. I knew no one would believe you if you discovered the truth. The previous babysitter was trouble. She had to go. Your lucky car accident happened at just the right time."

I gasped. "My *lucky* car accident?" I shrieked. "That accident *killed* my father!"

"But it brought you to me," she said softly. "And I knew you were just right."

"How can you do this?" I cried. "Harry is a killer. He killed two people, two kids from my school."

"Your fault," she said, sneering. "Your fault. You let him stay up late. Your fault entirely." She banged her fist on the tabletop. "So far, Harry is perfect. We had three failures. But Harry is perfect. And I'm going to protect him by sending you away for a long time."

"I don't think so," I said quietly, calmly.

She blinked. She studied me. "*What* did you just say?"

"I said, I don't think so, Dr. Shein. I don't think I'll be going anywhere. I think *you'll* be going away. Not me."

57.

Have you lost your mind?" Dr. Shein snapped. Her face twisted into a mask of anger.

"Did you really think I didn't figure out the truth about you?" I said. "*You* got me the job with Brenda. You said you knew Brenda from before. You had to know what she was doing with Harry."

"You don't know what you're saying, Lisa."

I shook my head. "Dr. Shein, do you see this phone on my lap? It's connected to an app called FaceTime. Do you know what that is?"

She suddenly turned pale. She drew her lips into a tight thin line.

"Yes, I know what FaceTime is," she muttered.

"Well . . . Captain Rivera and two other officers from the Shadyside police force are right outside that door." I pointed. "They're in your waiting room, and they just watched our whole conversation."

Dr. Shein murmured something under her breath. I couldn't hear it. But I could see the fear in her eyes.

"You just confessed," I said. "Now they'll be able to round up Harry and Brenda and Alice and Nate and Saralynn—and the three other pitiful creatures in those cages. And they'll be able to stop the horrible killings in this town."

That was quite a speech, and it left me breathless. I gripped the phone as if it were a life preserver.

I gasped as Dr. Shein let out a shrill, angry cry. She leaped up from her desk and bolted forward. She gave me a hard shove that almost sent me flying off the chair. Then she spun away from me, and her shoes thudded over the carpet as she ran out the office door—right into the arms of Captain Rivera and the other officers.

"Yesss!" I shouted, pumping my fists in the air. "Yes! Yes!"

I ran outside where my mother was waiting for me. She had tears in her eyes, and her cheeks were flushed. She tried to speak but she was too emotional to get any words out. Finally, she draped her good arm around my shoulders and whispered, "Let's go home."

EPILOGUE

I don't know how the police kept the real story out of the news.

Sure, everyone reported on the two murders. The story of the "Cannibal Killings" was all over town. And of course, people were horrified.

But they'd be even more horrified if they knew the murderer was a child-demon—that people were secretly raising a dangerous inhuman creature on Fear Street.

That story never made the news.

I guessed the police and the reporters decided it was better not to frighten the people of Shadyside. And maybe they didn't want any more scary stories about Fear Street going around.

Or perhaps they thought no one would believe them. After all, no one believed *me* . . . till the very end.

I could only guess the reason the story was hushed up. But I do know that Nate and Saralynn disappeared from school the day after I brought the police to Dr. Shein's office.

They were never seen again. No school announcement was made about them. The principal . . . the teachers . . . no one said a word.

A week later, I drove past Brenda's house on Fear Street. The house was dark. No sign of anyone inside. And Alice's house had a FOR SALE sign in the middle of the front lawn.

It felt strange to lose so many people who were in my life. I felt this weird combination of sadness and loss—and relief—at the same time.

I actually tried to phone Nate once. Yes, I knew he was part of a very evil conspiracy to raise a demon. I knew he had lied to me right from the start. I knew he wasn't who he pretended to be.

But Nate had saved my life. He had a last-minute change of heart and he stopped Brenda from killing me. He let me escape. So I had this crazy idea that I should call him and thank him for that.

But when I punched in the number, his phone didn't even ring. Just silence at the other end. "Dead silence," I murmured to myself. "Dead silence." I tried his number three times. Then I gave up.

"That's all over," I told myself. "I'm fine now. I'm putting that all behind me."

Yes, my life was definitely in a good zone. For one thing, I was enjoying my new after-school job.

I was lucky to get be hired as an assistant to the three full-time caregivers at the Wee Winners Daycare Center.

Most days after school we have fifteen to twenty kids with us. They're from four years old to ten, and we try to give each one a lot of attention.

"This is a better job for you," Mom said, the master of understatement.

"Mom, *any* job would be better than babysitting a demon!" I exclaimed.

"That's not what I meant," she insisted. "It's a good job for you because you're with other people. You're not sitting alone in a house, totally in charge of everything all by yourself."

I had to agree with her about that.

It was a good job for me, even on days like today when dealing with the kids was a challenge. I had to stop Jeremy's nosebleed, and two girls were having an angry tug-of-war over the same Dr. Seuss book, and Ivan (We call him Ivan the Terrible) refused to let anyone else have the iPad.

Mindy, the boss, had a dentist appointment. So it was just Carol and Audra and me, and even they were a little frantic since the kids all seemed to be having a very bad day.

I spotted a boy sitting by himself on the window seat in a corner. He held a large poster in front of him, and I couldn't see his face. "Roger? Is that you?" I called, making my way past the crafts table to him.

"Roger? Why are you all alone back here?" I asked.

He slowly lowered the poster. I stopped with a short intake of breath. And stared at the curly blond hair, the pink cheeks, the angelic round face, the adorable smile . . .

"Oh."

Stunned, I raised my hand to my mouth. "H-Harry!" I stammered. "Harry! What are you *doing* here?"

His smile grew wider. "I'm not Harry," he said softly. "My name is Sam."

He shot a hand out and wrapped it around my wrist. "My name is Sam," he repeated, tightening his grip until his fingers dug into my skin. "Will you be my friend? *Will* you? We can stay up late together."